"We'll jump toge

Brent uncurled Carly's ~~fingers from~~ the window frame.

Smoke cascaded over Carly as it poured through the open window. Her source of fresh air was now diminishing and the dizziness was becoming too much. She had to leave. She had no choice. Using Brent's hand as a leaning post, she carefully placed one foot on the outside ledge. Somewhere in her apartment, she heard her possessions burning up, popping and smashing with the high temperature. Her whole life was going up in flames because someone wanted to punish her for protecting children.

"We have to jump now," Brent said, pulling on her arm gently. "Before this window cracks."

Slowly, carefully, she lifted the other foot onto the ledge and squatted next to Brent, steeling herself to let go of the warm window frame.

"I'm scared," she said.

"Me, too." He grasped her hand and she wobbled on the ledge, but Brent held her firm. "On the count of three we jump together, okay?"

She nodded.

"One... Two... Three."

Elisabeth Rees was raised in the Welsh town of Hay-on-Wye, where her father was the parish vicar. She attended Cardiff University and gained a degree in politics. After meeting her husband, they moved to the wild rolling hills of Carmarthenshire, and Elisabeth took up writing. She is now a full-time wife, mother and author. Find out more about Elisabeth at elisabethrees.com.

Books by Elisabeth Rees

Love Inspired Suspense

Caught in the Crosshairs
Innocent Target
Safe House Under Fire
Hunted by the Mob
Uncovering Alaskan Secrets
Wyoming Abduction Threat

Navy SEAL Defenders

Lethal Exposure
Foul Play
Covert Cargo
Unraveling the Past
The SEAL's Secret Child

Visit the Author Profile page at LoveInspired.com.

WYOMING ABDUCTION THREAT

ELISABETH REES

LOVE INSPIRED SUSPENSE

INSPIRATIONAL ROMANCE

LOVE INSPIRED® SUSPENSE

INSPIRATIONAL ROMANCE

ISBN-13: 978-1-335-59934-6

Wyoming Abduction Threat

Copyright © 2024 by Elisabeth Rees

Recycling programs
for this product may
not exist in your area.

This is a work of fiction. Names, characters, places and incidents are either the
product of the author's imagination or are used fictitiously. Any resemblance
to actual persons, living or dead, businesses, companies, events or locales is
entirely coincidental.

For questions and comments about the quality of this book, please contact us
at CustomerService@Harlequin.com.

Love Inspired
22 Adelaide St. West, 41st Floor
Toronto, Ontario M5H 4E3, Canada
www.LoveInspired.com

Printed in U.S.A.

Whosoever therefore shall humble himself as this little child, the same is greatest in the kingdom of heaven. And whoso shall receive one such little child in my name receiveth me.

—Matthew 18:4-5

For my forever friend and partner in crime, Jane Thomas.

ONE

The chatter and laughter of the school children could be heard from the parking lot, and Sheriff Brent Fox picked up his pace, hoping he wouldn't be the last parent to collect their kids that day. The concrete beneath his feet shimmered with a slick wetness after a recent rain shower and he splashed in a puddle on the schoolyard, soaking the hem of his pants.

Beneath the covered shelter where the teachers stood with the children at the end of each school day, a high-pitched giggle rose up. Brent knew without even looking that it was five-year-old Ruby, his foster daughter. Sure enough, when he reached the shelter, she was standing next to her seven-year-old brother, Noah, with a hand clamped across her mouth, her shoulders rising and falling with laughter while her ponytails bounced in rhythm.

"Is that funny?" he asked in a playful voice,

bending down and tickling beneath her chin. "My sock is all wet now."

"Mine too!" Noah exclaimed. "I did the same thing at recess."

"Well, whaddya know?" Brent bumped a gentle fist on the boy's chest. "We're the wet sock buddies."

He looked up at Mrs. Hooper, Ruby's class teacher, and took off his hat. "Sorry if I'm a couple minutes late."

"You're right on time, Sheriff Fox," Mrs. Hooper replied. "You always worry about your timekeeping but you're one of the most punctual parents here at Pinedale Elementary."

"Glad to hear it." He stood up. "It's just that I'm eager to make a good impression on everybody at the school." He glanced down at the children and led Mrs. Hooper a few paces away to be out of their earshot. "Did somebody from the Department of Family Services contact you recently? My adoption caseworker said she'd be calling."

"Yes, I spoke to a very nice lady called Carly Engelman from Family Services today, and she told me she'd be sending us a questionnaire to complete regarding Noah's and Ruby's progress at school."

Brent raised an eyebrow. He wouldn't exactly use the word *nice* to describe Carly Engelman. He thought she was officious and impossible to please, and she was forcing him to jump through hoops to adopt the children he'd been fostering for nine months already. He assumed the paperwork would be a formality, but Ms. Engelman was making the process torturous, and he was only polite to her out of necessity.

"I'm not sure why it's taken eight months to get this far along," Brent said. "But I hope we're nearing the completion stage. I'd appreciate some honest feedback from you guys to support my application."

The teacher smiled broadly. "The school would be very happy to endorse you as a father, Sheriff. Those children have flourished under your care."

The praise buoyed him. "I can't pretend it's always been easy but it's rewarding." He fingered the brim of his hat awkwardly, always finding it painful to talk about the past. "Since my wife died, I worry that I might not be seen as a viable option for adopting."

Brent had been married to Tamsin when applying to foster, leading to the placement of Noah and Ruby in their home. But Tamsin had been involved in a tragic and fatal car accident just eight weeks afterward. He still struggled to breathe at times, wondering how on earth his perfect life had fallen apart in the blink of an eye.

Mrs. Hooper placed a reassuring hand on his shoulder. "We have plenty of wonderful single parent families in our school so you're in good company. Try not to worry."

"Thank you. I'm grateful for everything you've done for us."

Turning his attention back to Noah and Ruby, he extended his arms and they took a hand each, with Ruby skipping and jumping as always and Noah slightly more reserved. In the parking lot, the pair hopped into his truck and Brent buckled them into their seats, fielding the never-ending questions about what they could have for dinner, what TV shows they could watch and whether their bedtime was chosen by God. Noah figured that if God didn't choose his bedtime, then it could be moved to a later one. Brent smiled at the kid's smartness and told him that bedtime wasn't up for negotiation, not even with God.

Walking around the truck to the driver's door, he stopped for a moment to raise his face skyward and give thanks for this beautiful family he had acquired. Losing Tamsin seven months ago had hit him like a ton of bricks, but those kids gave him a reason to keep going. They meant the world to him. Of course, it helped matters that he was surrounded by the Wind River Mountains in the little town of Pinedale, Wyoming. That kind of rugged scenery could heal even the most scarred of hearts.

"It looks like you guys had a good day at school?" he said, settling into the seat and starting up the truck. "Did you paint a picture today, Ruby, because you seem to have painted your pants yellow?"

"I painted a picture of flowers," she said, raising her fists in the air like a champion. "They're called babies."

He laughed, pulling out onto Pine Street. "I think you mean daisies. I can't wait to see it."

"Mrs. Hooper put it out to dry on the—"

BANG! A car barreled into them at an intersection, hitting him with such speed and ferocity that he spun on the wet asphalt, tires screeching and vision swirling. As soon as they were motionless, he turned and checked on Noah and Ruby, strapped into their seats, their faces showing fear and confusion. They were unharmed, as was he, but the occupants of the other vehicle might not be so fortunate. He unclipped his radio from his shirt, exiting the vehicle to assess the scene.

"What in the—"

Heading his way was a trio of armed men, all dressed in black like bank robbers, each wearing a clown mask.

One of the men jerked his head toward Brent's truck and pushed an accomplice forward. "You get the kids and we'll deal with the sheriff."

Brent's blood ran cold and he swiveled on his feet to hurl himself back inside the truck to floor the gas pedal in an attempt to make a getaway. For some reason, these men had come for his foster children and he was outnumbered and outgunned. His best chance of protecting them was to get to the Sheriff's Department on the outskirts of Pinedale, where his deputies would provide a strong defense. Forcing the truck to its absolute limits, he sped out of town, his eyes flicking between the road ahead and the rearview mirror.

"All units, please respond," he said into his radio, noticing the black SUV looming behind him. "This is Sheriff Fox. I'm being pursued by three unknown assailants on Lake Road. They are armed and dangerous, wearing clown masks. I got my kids with me. Immediate assistance required."

BANG! His car was rammed again, this time from behind. Ruby screamed and Noah buried his head in his hands.

"It's okay," he called in a calming voice, as his driver's door flew open. The metal had been dented and warped by the sideways impact and it refused to click shut. He yanked it closed, praying it would hold long enough to get away. "Don't worry. Daddy's here. We'll be fine."

"What do they want?" Noah asked, still shielding his eyes.

"Try not to think about it," Brent said, despite being able to think about nothing else himself. "I'll keep you safe. I promise."

The engine whined against the power that Brent was demanding, and he hoped there was no damage beneath the hood. He couldn't grind to a halt on this quiet stretch where they'd be surrounded by nothing but open road and mountains.

The black SUV was now alongside him, swerving into the side of his truck, trying to force him off the road. He fought back, using the bulk of his truck to hold his ground, but the men were waving their guns, sending him a clear message. Why were they doing this to him? It was like a nightmare. His truck was being battered from the side and he silently prayed, offering his life in exchange for his foster children's. As he saw the window of the SUV slide down, he wondered if he would now have to make that sacrifice.

"Close your eyes, kids," he said. "Squeeze them tightly shut. I love you."

The noise of a siren filled the air and Brent's eyes snapped to his mirror. One of his deputies was in hot pursuit, racing toward the dueling cars with lights blazing. But the presence of backup didn't seem to faze the men in the SUV and they swiped Brent's truck with such force that he couldn't control his trajectory. His driver's door popped open again and he veered off the road. Skidding on the grassy edge near the shoulder, he hit a road sign and stopped abruptly. He jumped from the vehicle, pulled his gun and tried to take aim, but the SUV was coming straight for him, hurtling like a train. He had just enough time to dive across the hood of his truck as the SUV scraped along the metal, creating a horrible and prolonged crunching sound, ripping off his driver's door along the way.

Brent hauled himself from the ground, realizing that his gun had been knocked from his hand. He had no time to look for it, as a blow was delivered to his abdomen. He doubled over, but gritted his teeth through the pain, lashing out with his fists, feeling contact being made with hard and bony surfaces: a jaw, a nose, a shoulder. He heard the voices of Noah and Ruby calling out to him, with Ruby using the name she'd chosen as his moniker: Daddy Brent.

"No! No!" he called out, realizing that somebody was removing them from the car. "Leave them alone."

A shot rang out. The man he was grappling with suddenly lurched forward and fell to the ground with a thump, blood oozing from his torso.

Brent's deputy Amir Faisal stood at the side of the road, gun aloft and breathing hard. The shot had come from his weapon.

"Stay right where you are!" Deputy Faisal ordered. "And put down the children."

There by the crumpled SUV were the remaining two masked men, holding on to the hands of Ruby and Noah, with both children squirming to be released. Brent quickly located his gun in the grass and held it out front, a gesture that was immediately reciprocated by the would-be kidnappers. Now, all four men had guns trained on each other, remaining in a standoff for a few seconds before one of them spoke.

"If you let us take the children, nobody gets hurt."

Brent took a bold step forward. "Over my dead body."

Deputy Faisal backed him up. "Mine too. If you try to take those kids, one of us will make sure that you leave here in a bag."

The men exchanged a glance through their masks, communicating soundlessly with their eyes, before dropping the children's hands and backing away, keeping their guns trained on the officers until they were safely inside their battered SUV. Then, with a squeal of tires, they were gone, leaving the lifeless body of their accomplice behind on the grass.

Brent holstered his gun and rushed to the kids, enveloping them in his arms and checking them over, head to toe. The feel of their small arms around his neck filled him with horror and rage. Who would terrify little children like this?

His answer came quickly, as Noah spoke quietly. "I know one of those men. I recognize his voice."

Brent pulled away to cup the boy's cheek. "Who is he?"

"He's our daddy."

Brent sat in an armchair in his living room, still coming to terms with what had happened earlier that day. His ordinary, happy life had been upended and he had no words to describe his feelings of devastation.

"Noah and Ruby are doing fine," Amir said, sitting on the couch opposite. "Your mother is playing games with them upstairs and they're singing songs. Kids are resilient like that."

Brent really didn't want to face the stark reality of the danger that had visited them but he had no choice. "We have to get them into some kind of safe house until their birth father is caught. He'll try to kidnap them again."

The other deputy in the room, Liam Norton, spoke up in agreement.

"I second that, boss. Let's get them out of here this evening. We can ask the Sheriff's Departments in neighboring counties to cover our shifts so that Amir and I could come with you. You'll need all hands on deck."

"I should contact my caseworker and get her advice before doing anything. I don't want to jeopardize my adoption application."

Brent slid his cell from his pocket and scrolled to the phone number for Carly Engelman, while a knock sounded at the door. He watched Amir open up and speak to a police officer from the nearby town of Jackson, who handed over a brown envelope. Meanwhile, Ms. Engelman's phone rang and rang, finally going to voice mail. He'd have to try again in a little while.

"Hey, boss, you probably want to look at this," Amir said, handing him the envelope. "I just spoke to a police sergeant from Jackson, who told me that the black SUV was involved in a shoot-out with his officers about an hour ago. Two officers were wounded and the masked men escaped but they left behind some key evidence in the vehicle."

Brent opened the envelope and shook the contents onto the coffee table. He saw a number of photographs of Carly Engelman, clearly taken covertly while she went about her business. Alongside the photographs was a schedule of her daily routine, detailing exactly where she went and at what times. Brent knew that she had recently moved to Pinedale, and now lived in an apartment by the lumber store. A photo of that same apartment block was among the pile, an *X* marking her exact place of residence. And above the *X*, someone had scrawled the word TARGET in large red letters.

Brent felt the breath leave his body. "Carly Engelman is on their hit list." He jumped up from the chair. "We have to go warn her."

"I'll go." Amir grabbed his keys from the coffee table. "You stay with the kids."

"No." Brent held up a hand to stop him. "I should go. She can be a prickly character sometimes, and I'm the only one of us that knows her. It's probably best if I explain the situation." He plucked the keys from Amir's hand. "I'll try to persuade her to accompany me back here, and we'll discuss her options."

He headed for the door, praying she would be home. Because if she was being tracked on the road, he might not be able to get to her in time.

Carly closed the lid on her laptop and switched off her desk-side lamp with a satisfied smile. She had successfully completed the progress report for two small children whose case she was overseeing in the Department of Family Services. Noah and Ruby Odell were a couple of kids being fostered in the town of Pinedale, and now in the process of being adopted. Carly knew the kids well. She had been the caseworker responsible for removing them from their family home and finding them a foster placement with the sheriff of Sublette County and his wife, who had since sadly passed away.

Carly was used to dealing with harrowing

cases involving children. With eighteen years as a child protection officer under her belt, she thought that nothing could shock her. Yet, when she had found Noah and Ruby Odell, malnourished and clinging to each other for comfort, she had openly wept. Their mother was lying in bed, dead from an overdose, and their drug-dealer father was casually watching television as if he didn't have a care in the world. Lifting those little limbs into her arms had been one of the best and worst experiences of her life. She hated to see their suffering, yet she was overjoyed at being able to bring it to an end.

The children were now thriving under the care of Sheriff Fox and he had made an application to adopt them, but the process wasn't yet completed and would likely take quite a while longer. As a result, the sheriff was frustrated with her and they'd clashed on more than one occasion due to his impatience to be the children's legal father and change their surname to match his. He had expected the paperwork to simply be a formality, whereas she wanted to be certain of making the right decision. She'd made a bad call in the recent past that had resulted in fatal consequences. It was an incident that she rarely spoke about, not even with colleagues.

A car door slammed outside, and she went to the window to peer at the scene below her apartment. All was quiet on this wide, leafy street, in a town that she had instantly fallen in love with after moving there from the bustling capital city of Cheyenne. Pine-dale was exactly where she needed to be, with its sleepy atmosphere and folksy vibe. That one bad decision in Cheyenne five months ago had left deep emotional scars, so she had transferred to an office in nearby Rock Springs, reduced her hours and concentrated on healing her spirit. But since moving there a couple weeks ago, she'd been plagued by a sensation of being watched. A black SUV would often park outside her home and sit there all day, the tinted windows adding to its ominous air. A few times, she was sure she was being followed while getting lunch or running errands. It creeped her out.

"It's all in your head, Carly," she told herself, walking to the kitchen to make herself a meal. "You catch the bad guys, not the other way around."

The buzzer to the main apartment door downstairs began sounding in her hallway, with someone activating it over and over. She padded to her front door in her socks and pressed the button.

"Hello. Who's there?"

"It's Sheriff Brent Fox, Ms. Engelman. Can you buzz me in, please?"

Carly knitted her eyebrows together in confusion. She didn't have an appointment with Sheriff Fox until next week. And she never conducted client calls in her own home anyway.

"There's been a mix-up somewhere, Sheriff," she said. "We're not due to meet for another seven days."

"I know, but I'm here on a different matter."

It wasn't that she didn't trust Sheriff Fox, but she was drained of energy, hungry and tired.

"I'll come by the station tomorrow morning," she said. "At around nine, if that's okay."

"I need to see you now." He was insistent. "It's important."

A seed of worry planted in her belly at the change in his tone. "Okay. Come on up."

She pressed the button that would let him in on the first floor, before opening her apartment door and listening to the sheriff's sure and fast footsteps on the stairs, taking them two at a time. When he came into view, he was wearing his full uniform, minus the hat, and she couldn't prevent her eyes from running the full length of his physique. His shirt and pants fit just perfectly on his tall and muscular frame and creases were neatly pressed in all the right places.

He stopped at her apartment door and smiled. "Can I come inside?"

She realized that she was staring. "Oh! Sure. Of course."

Standing back to allow him to enter the hall, she noticed that his brown hair and beard were flecked with tiny traces of gray. At forty years of age, he was graying a little prematurely, but it suited him well. Some men were born to be silver foxes and Sheriff Fox was among them, not just because of the name.

"Would you like some coffee?" she asked, leading him into the kitchen. "I'd offer you dinner but it's not very exciting. I'm just about to make mac and cheese. Make yourself comfortable." She gestured to a chair.

"No thanks on dinner." He sat at her kitchen table and placed a brown envelope on the surface. "I'm afraid I'm here with some bad news. My car was run off the road earlier today and a kidnapping attempt was made on Noah and Ruby."

Her hand flew to her mouth. "What? How? Who? Are the kids okay?"

He patted the chair next to him and she

sat, her knee pressed against his under the small table.

He spoke slowly, as if wanting her to listen to every word. "The children are fine. They're with my mother and my deputies right now. I managed to repel the attack with help from Deputy Faisal, but one of the three assailants was shot and killed. I just got word on the radio that he's been identified as a known accomplice of Clarence Odell."

She gasped. "Noah and Ruby's father?"

"That's right. He tried to kidnap the children right from under my nose."

Carly stood up and began to pace the kitchen, shoving her hands into the large pocket of her hooded sweatshirt. "Are you sure it was him?"

"Yeah, Noah recognized his voice. I put out a warrant for his arrest this afternoon."

She sat down again and put a hand across her chest to calm her rapid heartbeat. She hadn't realized the lengths that Odell would go to in order to keep his children. The deadbeat dad had made a failed bid to gain custody of Noah and Ruby earlier this year. Carly's testimony at family court had been pivotal in blocking all visitations, and the judge had agreed to terminate Odell's parental rights. Odell had stared at her with bitter hatred throughout the proceedings, even making a surreptitious throat-slitting gesture at one point. He had blamed her for the fact that every single decision went against him.

"That's not everything you need to know," the sheriff said, opening up the envelope in his hands and sliding out some photographs. "It looks like he's got you in his crosshairs."

He placed three photographs onto the table and it took Carly a few seconds to realize that they were pictures of her, showing her getting into her car, leaving a courthouse and entering her apartment block. Odell had been following her for at least two weeks, building up a profile of her daily routines, no doubt working out the best way to launch an attack. She felt the color drain from her face and the sheriff took her hand to sandwich between his own.

"For your own safety, it's a good idea that you leave your apartment and come with me right away. I'm planning on moving the children to a new location tonight and I recommend that you come with us. I'll call Family Services and inform them of the situation without giving any details of your whereabouts. Hopefully, Odell will be captured very soon and we can return to normal." He flashed her a smile, but it didn't help lift her spirits. "We can stand to be roomies for a while, right?"

Carly thought of all the cases she was currently overseeing. Some involved child protection while others related to fostering and adoption. She couldn't abandon her responsibilities. Another child under her care might be seriously hurt, or worse.

"I can't leave my job without giving the department any warning," she said. "People are relying on me. Children need me."

"Wherever we go, I'll set up a secure internet connection so you can continue to work remotely."

"That's great and all, but what about court appearances or home visits?"

He squeezed her hand. "We'll find a way around it. I can accompany you on those visits or arrange a police escort. We're kind of flying blind at the moment, and my main concern is getting you out of here without delay. We know that Odell is on the warpath and he'll be agitated and frustrated after his failed kidnapping attempt. Noah and Ruby are currently under armed guard so I don't want him to take out those frustrations on you." He looked around the kitchen in her small, one-bedroom apartment. "You're an easy target here."

With each word that came from the sheriff's mouth, Carly became more fearful. Looking down at the photographs, she couldn't kid herself that Odell wasn't serious about making her suffer. He intended on taking revenge. A man like that could hold a grudge forever, especially against a strong woman.

"I'll pack a bag," she said, standing up. "How long will I be gone?"

"Let's assume it'll only be a few days. We can always return for more things if it extends beyond that."

She walked into her bedroom and pulled a suitcase from the top of her closet, her previous hunger now replaced with sickness. Sheriff Fox had no idea how long she'd be away from her home, because Odell's capture wasn't certain. She could be gone for days or weeks or even months. Thankfully, she didn't have children to consider. Her long-held decision to shun marriage and a family had proven to be a good one after all. How could she become a mother herself when so many defenseless kids like Noah and Ruby needed her to stand up for them? The Lord had called her to dedicate her life to children who suffered, and she was glad to do it, even when maternal longings occasionally caught her off guard.

She threw sweaters, jeans, underwear, pajamas and sweats into her case, and laid toiletries on top. Then she scraped her blond hair into a ponytail and secured it with an elastic, before pushing her feet into sneakers and shrugging on a padded coat. Wherever she was going, she didn't want to be cold.

Wheeling her case into the hallway, leaving indentations on her deep-pile carpet, she saw Sheriff Fox waiting for her, his expression one of concern and worry. She really didn't want to be sharing her personal space with a client, especially the sheriff. His frustration at the slowness of his adoption process was bound to rear its head again, and she refused to be put under pressure to speed things up. He'd have to learn some patience. She had resolved to make no more mistakes.

"You ready, Ms. Engelman?" he asked.

She smiled at the formality. "If we'll be roomies, I guess we should be on first-name terms."

"That's good with me. Are you ready, Carly?"

"I'll just get my laptop," she said, opening the door to her small study. "I can't go anywhere without that."

Dropping to the carpet, she unplugged the cable and wound it around her hand, while the sheriff picked up the laptop from the desk and slotted it into its case. He reached out his hand to help her stand and she took it, suddenly light-headed and woozy.

"You need to eat something," he said, holding her close to his chest while the black spots behind her eyes danced around. "I have some snacks in the car." He pulled away from her and lifted his nose into the air. "You don't have anything cooking in the oven, do you?"

She shook her head as a faint smell of smoke filled the small space around them. The sheriff darted from the room and into the hallway.

"We have to get out of here fast," he said. "Leave your things and let's go."

She dropped the laptop charger and ran to his side just as a huge whoosh sounded behind the door. Flames engulfed the front door, and an overpowering stench of gasoline filled her nostrils. Before them was a wall of fire, making it impossible to leave via the only exit route.

They were trapped.

TWO

Brent grabbed Carly's hand and pulled her into the room that was the farthest distance from the spreading fire. Once inside, he slammed the door shut and yanked the robe from the door hook to plug the gaps beneath. Then he pulled his cell from his pocket and called 911, telling the dispatcher they were trapped inside a building that had been set on fire using accelerant. The presence of gasoline would cause this fire to be superheated and volatile, making survival all the more difficult. With this in mind, Brent requested the fire department's air rescue cushion, knowing it was their most effective means of escape.

"My eyes are burning," Carly said, sinking the heels of her hands into the sockets. "The smoke hurts."

He pressed down on her shoulders. "Get on the floor where the air is cleaner." He pointed to a door in the corner. "What's behind that door?"

"A bathroom."

Entering the small bathroom, he grabbed a bunch of towels and placed them under the shower head to soak them with cool water. Then he returned to Carly and placed the towels around the bedroom's doorframe, while saving one for her face. Placing it over her mouth, he instructed her to breathe through the damp cotton. The thick, acrid smoke was filling the room quickly and he felt their surroundings growing hotter and hotter by the second.

"Brent." Carly took his hand. "I'm dizzy." She spoke in short puffs. "I think I might pass out."

"Don't lose consciousness," he said, holding the towel over her face. "Breathe slowly through your nose, okay? Stay calm and we'll get through this."

He crouched next to her, coughing into the crook of his elbow while straining to listen for the sounds of the fire truck heading their way. Finally, he heard the siren's wail bouncing through the streets, only a minute or two away. Carly was sagging in his arms, her head beginning to loll back and her eyelids flickering. He would not allow her to die in this smoke-filled apartment. Lifting her onto her feet and discarding the wet towel, he dragged her to the window and opened it, allowing the cool and clear air to revive her. She appeared to gulp the freshness, gagging and spluttering between breaths.

She gripped the fabric of his shirt tightly. "If I don't make it, please tell my parents that I wasn't scared."

"I don't want to hear that kind of talk." His own head was now beginning to feel woozy and he fought off the effects of smoke inhalation. "Two fire trucks are pulling up right now. The firefighters will inflate an air cushion on the ground below us."

"You jump first. You have foster kids to think about. I have nobody who depends on me."

He grabbed her around her waist and hoisted her onto the windowsill in readiness for climbing out the window. Meanwhile, smoke continued to swirl around them in thick, dark plumes.

"A ton of kids depend on you," he said. "So don't argue with me about who goes first."

Behind them, the fire now licked at the edges of the bedroom door, yellow and orange tendrils forcing their way inside. Opening the window had been necessary but had served to provide oxygen for the flames, and the heat was becoming oppressive. Beneath his shirt, Brent's skin tingled with sweat, and he leaned out the window to check on the progress of the air cushion. It was being dragged out onto the grass below the apartment alongside a huge air pump. He knew from his experience dealing with jumpers that these lifesaving inflatables took less than a minute to expand to full size.

"Hold up," he said, leaving her sitting on the windowsill while he darted to the bed to pick up her purse from the duvet. "I'm guessing there's important stuff in here."

She nodded. "My cell, my wallet, my keys."

"I'll drop it onto the cushion." He returned to her. "I hear it inflating so it's almost ready for us. All you need to do is step out onto the ledge and let go. Watch this."

He held the leather bag out of the open window and released his grip. It sailed through the air before being enveloped by the plastic pillow below.

"Look how easy that was," he said. "I can see a firefighter retrieving it right now." He smiled, trying to rally her courage. "The purse is just fine so we know it works. Now it's our turn."

She shook her head, eyes streaming from either smoke or fear. Or both. "I can't."

He heard the whooshing sound of the cushion maintaining its air content, having now reached its full capacity. "Yes, you can. Come on, let's go."

She remained frozen. "I really can't. I'm scared of heights."

Carly gripped the edges of the window-sill, her eyes burning and her throat stinging. She'd always been afraid of heights, ever since she was a girl, and the thought of hurling herself into thin air caused her limbs to seize, as if she had no control over them. Even though she was surrounded by smoke and watching flames force their way farther and farther into her bedroom, she still couldn't move.

"It's only fifty feet," Brent said. "You can do it. You *have* to jump."

"I can't."

"If you don't jump, then neither do I."

She coughed and coughed as a dense black plume surged toward the window. Soon the entire room would be engulfed, and if she didn't move from that place, she'd be condemning Brent to die alongside her. Reaching up to grip the edges of the window frame, she placed her foot on the sill and tried to haul herself up. Her legs were shaky and she slipped, but Brent caught her in his arms and lifted her back into position.

"Put one foot out onto the ledge outside," he said, holding her hand tight. "Don't look down yet."

But that's exactly what she did. Below the window was a huge, white cushion, marked with a red cross in the center. She let out a yelp and closed her eyes, crouched on the inside sill, vertigo setting in and making the ground seem like a hundred miles away instead of fifty feet. The bedspread in the room caught fire and crackled as the flames took hold of the cotton, filling the air with curling and swirling pieces of red-hot fabric.

"I'll go first and lead you out." Brent put his hands on the window frame and dragged his body through, placing both feet on the ledge outside, scooching along the thin plastic shelf backward to give her room to exit.

"Come on," he said. "We'll jump together. I'll hold you."

Smoke cascaded over Carly as it poured through the open window. Her source of fresh air was now diminishing and the dizziness was becoming too much. She had to leave. She had no choice. Using Brent's hand as a leaning post, she rose from her crouched position and carefully placed one foot on the outside ledge. The entire window frame was warm as she hugged it, half in and half out of the apartment. The fire seemed to have super-heated the entire building. Somewhere in her apartment, she heard her possessions being burned up, popping and smashing with the high temperature. Her whole life was going up in flames because someone wanted to punish her for protecting children.

"We have to jump now," Brent said, pulling on her arm gently. "Before this window cracks."

Slowly, carefully, she lifted the other foot onto the ledge and squatted next to Brent, steeling herself to let go of the warm window frame.

"I'm scared," she said.

"Me too." He uncurled her fingers from the frame and she wobbled on the ledge, but Brent held her firm. "On the count of three, we jump together, okay?"

She nodded.

"One…two…three."

With a silent and jumbled prayer to God, Carly gripped Brent's hand and hurled her-self forward, letting out a scream of terror that didn't subside until they both sank into the soft and yielding cushion of plastic with their limbs entwined.

* * *

Brent toweled his hair while sitting on his bed, wearing a clean T-shirt and jeans. Despite scrubbing himself under a hot shower for twenty minutes, the pungent smell of smoke still seemed to cling to his skin, and he thought he'd never be rid of it. After falling onto the rescue pillow, he and Carly had been checked over by a paramedic at the scene and medically cleared to leave. They had waited until the fire crew announced that every resident was safely evacuated before driving to Brent's home. It now appeared they'd have to stay the night there, as the children had been put to bed by their grandmother and were sleeping soundly. Brent's plan to leave town would have to wait until the following day. At least his mother had returned home safe and well, having been accompanied by another of his deputies. That was one less person to worry about protecting. He was beginning to feel that he was spreading himself too thin.

He heard voices in the hallway downstairs and headed out onto the landing, bumping into Carly on the way. Like him, she was freshly showered, and her hair was wet, creating little damp patches on the red T-shirt that she wore over blue jeans. Brent had kept a few of Tamsin's old clothes in the closet after she died. He thought that one day Ruby might call them vintage and want to wear them. But right now, Carly was in dire need of them. She was a little taller than Tamsin had been and the hemlines on the jeans were above her ankles, but the fit was otherwise perfect. It was only just occurring to him that Carly was a naturally beautiful woman. At their adoption appointments, she always wore her hair scraped back and clothes that didn't draw attention to herself, so he'd never really looked at her before. With her blond hair cascading across her slim shoulders and her green eyes wide and moist, she looked like a Viking princess. It was the first time a woman's beauty had caught his attention since Tamsin died.

"The fire chief is here," she said, jerking her head toward the stairs. "I heard him tell one of your deputies that the apartment fire is finally out."

"Well, that's one bit of good news." On seeing her downcast expression, he rubbed her shoulder. "Maybe something can be salvaged from it. You never know."

She looked around at the closed doors around them, her eyes landing on Ruby's room, where her name was painted onto a unicorn-themed plaque.

"Is it a good idea to advertise where your foster children sleep?" she asked. "If somebody entered the house with the intention of committing a kidnapping, it's like a big red arrow pointing them in the right direction."

He bristled at the comment. Was she already judging his parenting even after being there for just a couple of hours? Would this be a running theme perhaps?

"We have three law enforcement officers here. Nobody is getting through to Ruby's room."

"You can't know that for sure. Have you considered passing this case along to the FBI? They'd be sure to have more resources than you do. I'm really worried for the children's safety."

"Attempted kidnapping isn't a federal crime so the FBI won't get involved." He pointed to his face. "Besides, there's nobody better than their father to protect them."

"Foster father," she corrected. "We haven't completed the legal paperwork yet."

"Yeah, and whose fault is that?" He was failing to keep his emotions from bubbling over. "I've done everything you've asked and more besides. I'm beginning to think you're just stalling because you don't think I'm good enough."

"I've been working in Child Protective Services for eighteen years, Brent, and I know my job inside out. I can't afford to rubber-stamp adoption applications, no matter how good an adoptive parent appears. What would happen if I made a mistake on an adoption? Have you thought about that? Every decision I make has a consequence, and that's why I need to be thorough."

Brent took a step backward, caught off guard by her passionate and slightly manic defense of her methods.

He decided to be bold. "*Did* you make a mistake on an adoption?"

She held his gaze for a good five seconds. "I don't discuss my work with anybody."

Brushing past him, she walked to the stairs and left him standing there alone, muttering under his breath. "I guess I'll take that as a yes."

Brent shook hands with Fire Chief Norman Davis, who had declined to sit because he was marked with soot and dirt from head to toe. Instead, he stood by the window, in front of the closed drapes, holding a clipboard that held a preliminary fire report and a sketch of Carly's apartment block. Amir and Liam were standing guard at the back and front doors, allowing Brent to breathe easy and share the burden of protecting both his family and Carly.

"This fire was one of the fiercest we've ever dealt with here in Pinedale," the chief said. "A lot of gasoline was used. And I mean a *lot*. There was absolutely no way anybody could've gotten out of that apartment via the stairwell, because the carpet was saturated with the stuff. My men couldn't get inside Ms. Engelman's apartment for at least an hour due to the intense heat."

Carly was curled up on the large armchair, her feet tucked beneath her. "You said that everyone in the block got out though, right?"

"For sure. We were able to reach them with ladders and rescue equipment. Your location was the most serious because your apartment door had been specifically targeted. The rescue cushion was definitely the right call. A few minutes after you jumped, that whole room was an inferno and the window smashed under the heat."

Brent saw Carly take a jerky inhalation. Much like her, he didn't like imagining what might've been. His children had already lost their foster mother. The last thing they needed was to lose their foster father too. And, of course, he had just been reminded of his status as a foster father, rather than a court-appointed, adoptive one. It was as if Carly was putting him in his place, making it clear that the adoption was far from being finally okayed. It had hurt him at the time, but he was determined not to let the comment fester. There were too many other problems to face.

"What's the likelihood of getting any forensic evidence from the scene, Norm?" he asked.

The chief puffed out his cheeks. "Oh boy, that's a tall order. Arson attacks are always difficult to investigate because any evidence is literally burned up. We rarely recover fingerprints, fibers or DNA from scenes like this. Our best shot at catching this guy is analyzing security footage. If I can get a good facial shot of the arsonist, you can run it through your database, huh, Sheriff?"

Brent exchanged a glance with Carly, who was no doubt thinking the same thing as he was.

"We think we know who set the fire," he said. "But I'd like to be able to add this crime to his arrest warrant."

"We'll do our best, but don't hold out much hope. That apartment block has been incinerated. There's nothing left except ash."

Brent saw Carly drop her head into her

hands, and he made a gesture to end the discussion, but the fire chief was on a roll and didn't pick up the signal.

"It's as if somebody wanted to destroy literally everything in the place," he continued. "A real scorched-earth mindset. I've seen some devastation in my career, but this is on another level. Everywhere you look there's blackened and twisted—" He stopped, suddenly noticing Brent's frantic hand movements. "Ah, well, you get my drift. I wanted to come tell you that the building will be cordoned off so nobody is allowed in or out."

"That's fine by me, Chief," Carly said. "There's nothing to go back for anyway."

"I'm truly sorry, Ms. Engelman. Your apartment suffered the worst of the fire, but you got out. I thank God that you're sitting here, safe and well."

She shot him a small smile. "I'm not sure that God had much to do with it, Chief. It was Sheriff Fox who got me out. He deserves all the praise."

Brent pointed his finger upward. "All my courage comes from the Lord, so I guess you could call it a joint effort."

"Call it what you like," she said, downcast. "God and I aren't exactly on speaking terms right now."

Taking his cue to leave, the fire chief moved toward the door, nodding a goodbye to Carly along the way.

"I'll get back to the scene and make sure everything is secured," he said. "The Arson Investigation Team from Cheyenne will visit tomorrow and we'll keep you posted on the progress. Goodnight, both of you. You'll be in my prayers."

"Thank you, Norm," Brent said, shaking his hand. "I appreciate all that you're doing."

He then directed the chief into the hallway, where Amir would unlock the front door and ensure it was relocked afterward. If Brent intended on leaving for a safe house tomorrow, there was a lot to plan. His deputies would need to return home to pack some things, Carly would require some new clothes, the school would have to be informed of the children's temporary absence, and most importantly Brent needed to make a decision about where they'd go. But before all of that, there was an important conversation he wanted to have with Carly.

Returning to the living room, he dropped to one knee by her armchair. "You okay? Hungry? Thirsty?" When she shook her head, he added, "Angry?"

She laughed and let her head loll back onto

the seat cushion. For a moment she appeared to be carefree, but it didn't last long because her face suddenly broke. Her lips wobbled and her eyes filled with tears, which she quickly flicked away with an index finger.

"Yeah, I'm angry," she said. "Moving to Pinedale was meant to be a fresh start for me after what happened in Cheyenne." She stopped and adjusted her position awkwardly, and he didn't press her for details. "I've dedicated my entire life to taking care of vulnerable children and I guess I expected some kind of reward." She shook her head as if she'd selected the wrong choice of word. "Maybe not a reward exactly, but to enjoy a quiet life at the very least. I didn't expect to be thrown to the wolves."

"Who's thrown you to the wolves?" he asked, suspecting he knew the answer already.

"God."

He felt the heavy weight of the pain she appeared to be carrying. In spite of their differences, he wanted to help her heal and strengthen her faith.

"If you've been thrown to the wolves, then you've landed in the right place." He put a hand on her knee and flashed her a grin. "Because we're a trio of alphas so we get to lead the pack."

* * *

Carly knew that Brent was trying to make her feel better by joking around, but it was having a limited effect. Her beloved little apartment was nothing more than a smoking pile of ash, and every single possession she owned was gone. How could God abandon her like this when she needed Him most?

After making her adoption case mistake five months ago, she'd prayed more fervently than ever before, begging God to make the guilt and hurt go away. She'd felt His guiding hand leading her to Pinedale, where she could put the pain of the past behind her. The town was ideal, with its magnificent backdrop of the Wind River Mountain Range, hiking trails, rivers and lakes, cozy cabins and quaint stores that came with good, old-fashioned service. She had settled in quickly, thanking God for taking her to a place of such tranquility. She had even begun to contemplate the possibility of raising her own family there, which had taken her by surprise.

Yet, as quickly as God had shown her mercy, He'd snatched it away again. And now she was cowering from danger, stuck in a house with Sheriff Brent Fox while he pressured her to speed up an adoption process that filled her with dread. Noah and Ruby's case was the first one she had overseen since that of eight-year-old Laurie Stephens back in Cheyenne, and she had decided it would be her last. Carly had matched Laurie with a wonderful couple from the city, both of whom were doctors in a local hospital. They were financially secure, well educated and came with a ton of recommendations. They'd seemed perfect, and Carly had hurried along the adoption process to give Laurie the family she deserved ASAP.

But she had missed the red flags, and Laurie had paid the ultimate price for that error.

"Just ignore me," she said to Brent. "I'm feeling sorry for myself, that's all."

"You're allowed to cut yourself some slack. Nobody expects you to bounce back from a day like today."

Carly thought of all the children she'd come into contact with over the years. They'd managed to cope with hardships, showing the kind of strength and resilience that grown-ups rarely displayed. Adults could sure learn a thing or two from children about digging deep.

"I can't help but feel that…" She couldn't finish the sentence as a lump caught in her throat.

"Feel what?" His tone was gentle and soothing. "I promise not to judge."

"I feel like I'm being punished," she said. "Maybe God is letting me know that He's not pleased with me."

Brent shook his head. "God doesn't work like that. I promise. He forgives us when we do wrong. If you feel like He's punishing you, it's probably because you haven't forgiven yourself."

She stared at him, feeling horribly exposed. She didn't want anybody in Pinedale to know about what had happened, least of all Brent. How could he have any faith in her if he knew that she'd placed a child in a home where she subsequently lost her life?

"Like I said, just ignore me." She rose from the couch and headed into the hallway. "I'm gonna turn in for the night. I'll feel better after a good night's sleep."

"I'll be working on a rotating system with Liam and Amir. Two of us will be on guard duty at all times, so you can feel totally safe."

She smiled weakly. Nobody was ever totally safe. Not really.

"Thank you," she said. "For everything you're doing. I guess Noah and Ruby will be surprised to see me in the morning. How will we explain my presence here?" She pulled a face. "We don't want them getting any crazy ideas about you and me, right?"

"I'll tell them that it's all part of the adoption process. They'll probably be happy to see you because they're as impatient as I am to get this done."

Carly felt a tiny tug of irritation. "Did you already tell them the adoption is a sure thing?"

He folded his arms. "Not exactly, but they're obviously excited about me becoming their official new daddy. You know what a deadbeat their old one was."

"You can't make them any promises, Brent," she said sternly. "There are a lot of steps to complete before the paperwork gets stamped."

"Yeah, I think you mentioned that already." He was obviously exasperated. "What steps are you talking about exactly? I've already completed the home studies, attended the training and submitted my references. You've also asked the school for a report. What else is left to do?"

"I haven't yet finished the checks on you. There could be something lurking in your past that I'm not aware of."

"Carly, I'm the sheriff of Sublette County. What do you think I might be hiding? Bodies under the floor?"

She shot him a terse and tight-lipped smile.

"Very funny. All I'm saying is that it's dangerous to count your chickens."

"Okay." He put his hands in the air in apparent submission. "No chickens will be counted by me."

With a frosty atmosphere having descended over the room, she said good-night and made her way to the guest bedroom, where she knew she would toss and turn all night.

As she'd suspected, Carly had trouble sleeping. Every time she closed her eyes, she saw a wall of fire and heard the crackling of her furniture being eaten by flames. Odell had certainly made sure she was well and truly trapped in that inferno. He must've been watching the place when Brent arrived and decided to kill two birds with one stone. But he hadn't counted on Brent's determination to get them both out of there alive. Had Odell been on the sidelines with the other onlookers, she wondered, watching her being given oxygen and checked over by paramedics? Had he already been plotting his next attempt even at that moment? One thing was certain: he despised her.

Odell's court application petitioning for custody of Noah and Ruby made clear that he blamed Carly for tarnishing his reputation and undermining his status as a father. He claimed that he'd had no idea the children's mother had overdosed in the bedroom and was also unaware of the children being scared, cold and hungry. He'd had the audacity to present himself as a victim of an unfair system in which jumped-up caseworkers like Carly denied fathers their rights to take care of their children. Thankfully, the judge had sided with her and handed permanent custody of the children to Wyoming Family Services.

She threw back the covers on her bed and stood up, being reminded of the fact that she was wearing a dead woman's pajamas. It was sweet of Brent to loan her Tamsin's things, but she'd be purchasing her own clothes as soon as possible. Hopefully, this arrangement wouldn't last long anyway. Their relationship would suffer under this forced proximity, and she wanted to keep a professional distance.

Padding into the hallway, she headed for the bathroom, resisting the urge to check on the children. She might wake and scare them. Clicking on the light in the bathroom, she ran the faucet until the water turned warm, and filled the sink. Then she plunged her hands into the water and rinsed her face, rubbing the smoky soreness away from her eyes. Patting her skin dry with a soft towel, she appraised herself in the mirror, thinking that she had aged ten years in that one day. She had always looked much younger than her true age, but at that moment she felt every single one of her thirty-eight years resting on her face.

"I'm tired, Lord," she said. "And I trusted You to give me some rest."

An owl hooted outside and a breeze rushed through the tree in the yard. She raised the blind a couple of inches and peered into the darkness, while reaching up to pull the cord and switch off the light to give her a clearer view. She just wanted to reassure herself that she was safe before returning to bed. But a shaking of foliage in the bushes at the back of the yard caught her eye, the kind of movement that could only be created by a living creature. With a start, she sprang back from the window, clutching the collar of her borrowed plaid pajamas.

The respite that she badly needed was not about to come anytime soon. Something or somebody was lurking in the shadows.

THREE

Brent sat in the kitchen next to the back door in the midnight silence. Outside, an owl hooted at regular intervals, and the wind rustled the trees and bushes. His senses were heightened, tuned into each and every sound in the vicinity, in case one of them signaled danger. He gave a start as Liam crept into the kitchen, gun in hand and finger pressed against his lips. He was clearly spooked, and Brent immediately responded, jumping up from his chair and drawing his own weapon. Liam went to the window and pulled back the blind, peering out into the yard.

"Something's out there," he whispered. "In the bushes. Carly just reported that she saw it from the bathroom window. Might be a fox or a cat, but there's definite movement."

"Where's Carly now?"

"I told her to go back to her room and stay there."

"Good. Go wake Amir in the basement and guard both doors while I go see what's out there." Brent double-checked the bullets in the chamber and turned the lock on the door. "Secure the door behind me and do not leave this house under any circumstances. Call for backup if you need it, but your job is to protect the children and Carly, not me. Got it?"

"I got it, boss," Liam said, heading to the basement. "You've told me a million times already."

Through the small window in the door, Brent scanned the yard, his heart racing. He had drummed into his deputies that he should be on the very bottom of the list when it came to saving lives. As a father, his job was to put his children first. As a sheriff, his job was to safeguard Carly. He would lay down his life for either.

Seeing Amir and Liam enter the kitchen, Brent gave them the signal and made his move. He grabbed a flashlight from the counter, opened the door and stepped quickly into the cold, damp air. Remaining on the patio with his back against the wall for a few moments, he gave his eyes a chance to adjust to the inky blackness, before skirting along the sides of the yard toward the thick foliage of the cypress bush along the back wall. The leaves were shaking in the center, indicating that the movement was being created by something of considerable size. This certainly wasn't a cat or a fox.

Once he was close enough, Brent raised both his gun and his flashlight. "This is Sheriff Fox. Come out with your hands where I can see them."

He waited. The rustling and movement ceased. Yet no response was made.

"If you cooperate, you'll come to no harm," he continued. "Don't make this hard on yourself."

The bush began to shake violently as the person hiding among the leaves moved low and quick in the dense foliage, heading for the fence that divided Brent's yard from his neighbors'. Quick as a flash, a man in black jumped from the bush onto the pine slats and hauled his legs over the top. Brent holstered his gun and gave chase.

Vaulting the fence, he dropped his flashlight but maintained a visual on the suspect by tracking his silhouette. The man bounded across the neighboring lawn, avoiding a playset and sandbox, before springing up onto the next dividing boundary. The guy appeared to be small and wiry with an athletic ability that forced Brent to work hard to keep pace. They jumped fence after fence, the guy kicking aside lawn chairs and kids' toys as he sprinted through other people's properties. Finally, they reached a dead end, where the fence at the end of the street extended at least ten feet into the air. It was far too high to climb. The only way out of this yard was via the path at the side of the house, and Brent made sure to stand firmly in the way, pulling his gun to take aim.

Standing only a few feet apart, Brent could now see that the intruder was Clarence Odell. He recognized the pockmarked face from photographs. And Odell was now doubled over with exertion, gasping for breath. Brent couldn't see a gun in his possession, but that didn't mean he wasn't armed.

"Stay right there," Brent said between gulps of air. "Hands in the air."

Odell straightened up and stared at Brent, his expression a mix of anger, fear and hatred. Yet, a smile quickly spread across his face when the sound of an opening door punctuated the silence. In his peripheral vision, Brent saw a shaft of light cascade across the grass, and a voice called out from the property.

"Is that you, Sheriff?" It was his elderly neighbor, Wesley Evans. "I heard a noise and went to get my gun. Do you need any help?"

"Go back inside, Wes," Brent called, unwilling to take his eyes off Odell. "Lock your door and stay there."

Brent waited for the shaft of light to disappear, but it remained. Meanwhile Odell began to bounce from foot to foot as if preparing for an escape. The presence of a civilian complicated matters.

Brent called out the order once more. "I told you to go back inside, Wes."

"This is my yard," Wesley replied, his voice sounding worryingly close. "And I'm entitled to defend it."

With a quick look to his right, Brent saw his neighbor standing a few feet away in his bathrobe and slippers, a gun in his hand. That split-second glance was all it took for Odell to seize the opportunity to barrel into Brent with flailing arms, knocking his gun from his grip and sending him hurtling to the damp grass. There they wrestled, Odell's thin and contorting limbs proving difficult for Brent to pin down. Meanwhile, Brent was conscious of his neighbor's agitated presence next to them, his gun trained on both men. He prayed that Wesley wouldn't try to take a shot.

But he did take a shot. Into the air. The bullet cracked the sky, so loud and sudden that Brent released his grip on Odell, who jumped up and disappeared down the side of the house in the blink of an eye. Brent remained sitting on the grass and put his head in his hands, deciding that giving chase would be too dangerous after the discharge of a firearm. He knew that some of his neighbors would now want to investigate the commotion, most likely with a gun in hand. And Brent didn't want to place them in danger.

"What did you do that for, Wes?" he asked. "I was just getting the upper hand."

"I thought it might shock him enough to force him to give up."

"It shocked *me* enough to let him get away." Brent hauled himself to his feet and wiped the seat of his pants. "And that gunshot will have woken the whole neighborhood, so we can expect plenty of calls to the switchboard." His eyes traveled to Wesley's gun. "And some folks will grab their firearms and head outside just like you."

Wes rubbed his bald head. "Sorry, Sheriff. I thought I was helping."

"Don't worry about it." Brent patted his neighbor's shoulder. "We all make mistakes. Next time, follow my orders, okay? Now, go inside and lock your door."

He retrieved his gun from the grass and headed back home, where he'd direct the night shift deputies to scour the area for any sign of Odell. But deep down, he knew they'd never find a trace of him.

Brent sat at the kitchen table just as dawn was breaking. He was holding a security camera, retrieved from the bush in his yard, discarded by Odell in his haste to escape. Brent turned the device over in his hands, smoothing the blemish-free plastic. This camera was clearly brand-new, purchased with the sole intention of spying on Brent's home in order to give Odell feedback on their movements. It wasn't a particularly expensive camera, the same kind that people use on their doorbells, but it would be effective in analyzing their routines, capturing the times when the house was quiet and showing when lights were switched on and off.

Putting down the camera, he picked up the more concerning item that had been left behind by their intruder: an audio listening device. This little microphone, encased in black plastic that was no bigger than a matchbox, had been stuck beneath his patio table, ready to activate as soon as it detected voices. It was only thanks to a diligent search by Liam that the device had been found, leading them to be supercautious about what they said, in case others lurked nearby. The range of these devices could be powerful so they couldn't afford to take any chances.

Carly entered the kitchen, still wearing Tamsin's old pajamas and robe, her hair pressed down on one side and her eyes showing evidence of a poor night's sleep. Seeing her in the red plaid pajamas and fleecy robe brought back memories of lazy Saturday mornings spent with Tamsin, watching movies or making cookies. He had always known that she wasn't able to have children. She'd been honest with him right from their very first date, but it hadn't mattered. He was prepared to sacrifice anything to be with her. After ten years of marriage, she'd been the one to suggest fostering, and she'd wanted to offer a home to a brother and sister. Tamsin had hoped that she and Brent could move forward with an adoption if the kids settled and were happy. Sadly, she never got to see the end result of that plan, and now it was left to Brent to bring it to fruition on his own. Only Carly Engelman stood in his way.

"You look like you didn't get much sleep," he said, rubbing his own weary eyes. "How are you feeling?"

She filled a glass of water at the sink and turned to lean against it while she sipped.

"I feel like I've been run over by a truck."

"Yeah, sleep deprivation will do that to you. I sometimes wish we could all sleep like children." He pointed to the ceiling, above which Noah and Ruby were still in their beds and completely unaware of the overnight drama. "Life is very uncomplicated when you're a kid."

She sat at the table. "Except life isn't uncomplicated for Noah and Ruby, is it? Their father is trying to kidnap them."

"Odell is *not* their father," he said, looking her in the eye.

She nodded. "You're right. I should've said birth father."

Brent bristled at this sacred word being applied to Odell even in a biological capacity. "He doesn't deserve that label in any way, shape or form. I'm Noah and Ruby's father."

"I'm not getting into this again, Brent." She rose and walked to the sink to wash her glass. "The adoption process is still ongoing."

He sighed, unable to prevent himself from picking at this emotional wound.

"When I started the fostering process nine months ago, you were much more positive about the kids being adopted by me in the long term. I know that Tamsin has died since then, but I'm still the same person. I still love them with my whole heart. What's changed? Why do you seem like a different person now?"

She bent her head so that her hair fell across her face. "I'm not different."

"Yes, you are. You're way more bureaucratic now. You keep finding more forms to sign, and papers to check, and rules to follow. It's like you suddenly decided to throw up all these roadblocks. Why? Is it because I'm now a single parent applicant? Or did I do something to upset you?"

She pulled her hair off her face and held it back in a ponytail with her fingers, her eyes closed. "I'm just doing things by the book." When she opened her eyes, a flicker of pain swept across them. "I'll go get showered and dressed. I guess we'll be leaving today."

He shook his head and held up the listening device. "I can't talk about that."

"Okay." She seemed relieved to be able to bring the conversation to a close. "I'll come back down for breakfast."

She left the kitchen and Brent began to assemble a variety of foods on the counter to cook. He wanted to ensure that they had a hearty meal inside them for the day ahead. As he retrieved pans from the overhead hooks, he thought about Carly's assertion that she was simply playing by the book. She was lying to him. The change in her personality must be obvious, even to her, prompted by something she refused to share. Whatever the reasons for her new and difficult temperament, Brent was determined to play by her rules, obey all her commands and finish the process. And then he could happily avoid her for the rest of his life.

Carly sat at the breakfast table with Brent, Noah, Ruby and Amir. Liam was walking the perimeter of the house, searching for any more cameras or audio devices. A sweep of the interior had revealed nothing untoward, meaning they were safe to talk openly. Even so, Brent had given Carly strict instructions to not mention their nighttime intruder in front of the children. Hence, she had painted on her best happy face, despite feeling desolate inside. Brent's questions early that morning had hit home. She hadn't realized that she'd allowed the death of Laurie to have such a noticeable effect on her, but Brent had clearly identified a change in her attitude in recent months. She was no longer sure of herself and didn't think positively. And she had no idea how to rid herself of this negative state of mind.

Brent had prepared a huge breakfast table, with eggs, sausages, bacon, pancakes and coffee. She ate hungrily, realizing that this was her first proper meal since yesterday at lunchtime, and she noticed two pairs of little eyes staring at her the whole time. Noah and Ruby had been told that Carly was staying in their home temporarily as part of the adoption process, but they were still curious. Ruby, especially, paid close attention to Carly's every movement.

"Your hair is pretty," the little girl said. "It's like the yellow straw at the petting zoo."

Carly burst out laughing, quickly followed by the rest of the table.

"She *did* say it was pretty," Brent said, regaining his composure. "But you might want to steer clear of any horses today in case they try to take a bite out of you."

Carly put a hand up to her hair, which was still damp and unbrushed after her shower. "Thank you for the compliment, Ruby," she said. "Your hair is pretty too. I like your ponytails."

Ruby shook her head from side to side. "They're swishy. See?"

"Maybe you can help me brush my hair and make it look like yours. Yellow straw is nice, but I like swishy hair better."

"Don't let her brush your hair," Noah interjected, his inquisitive blue eyes exactly the same color as his sister's. "She hurts."

Ruby was indignant and screwed up her face. "I do *not* hurt. I'm gentle." She made brushing motions through the air with her hand. "Like this."

Noah rolled his eyes, which Carly suspected was a well-practiced move, designed to infuriate his sister. It had the desired effect, as Ruby reached for Brent.

"Daddy Brent," she said in a high-pitched voice. "Noah is making mean eyes at me again."

Carly smiled. It was undoubtedly a big deal for Brent to be called Daddy, even if his first name was used alongside. She could see that it meant a lot to him. She concentrated on telling herself that this family match was perfect. Brent would never harm these children.

"Let's all be nice to each other," Brent said, taking Ruby's hand and squeezing it while throwing an admonishing look Noah's way. "Because we're going on a little vacation for a few days. That'll be nice, huh?"

The children squealed and raised their arms in the air, cheering in unison.

"Where are we going, Brent?" Noah asked, making it clear that the older sibling hadn't yet reached the same comfort zone as his sister, and did not call him Daddy.

"It's a secret, but Liam, Amir and Carly are coming along too." He winked at Carly and her spine tingled. "So I want to see your best behavior in front of our guests, okay?"

Noah placed an index finger on his chin as if a thought had just occurred to him. "What about school?"

"I called your principal and she said that it's okay to take a few days' vacation time. We'll pack your things after breakfast and leave when the clock hits ten."

Ruby slipped off her seat and began jumping up and down, her ponytails bouncing. "I want to take my dolls and my cars and my books and my music box."

"Whoa!" Brent held up a hand. "Just some clothes and your favorite toy, okay?"

Amir checked his watch. "I could go make a start right away if it helps." He turned to the children. "You want Uncle Amir to come help you pack?"

Already excited about the prospect of a vacation, the children were halfway to the hallway door even before he'd finished the question, and Amir rose from the table.

"If you hear me begging for mercy, send reinforcements," he said with a smile. "Last time I watched the kids, they tied me up with a jump rope."

Alone with Brent, Carly was awkward and uncomfortable. He was starting to have an odd effect on her, making her want to run from the room and away from his scrutiny. She was worried that he might try to encourage her to discuss deep emotions, and that would lead to disaster. Once a brick was taken out of her wall, it could lead to the whole structure collapsing. Hence, she now made attempts to keep the conversation light.

"It's great that the kids are relaxed and happy with Amir," she said. "They call him uncle, huh?"

"They call all my deputies uncle," he replied. "It's like they suddenly got a whole new extended family through my work." He started to stack the dishes. "I'm a firm believer in the motto that it takes a community to raise a child."

"Me too."

He opened his mouth to speak and she readied herself for the inevitable probing questions about the adoption, but he promptly shut it again, clearly having a change of heart. Then he took the dishes to the kitchen counter and began stacking the dishwasher.

"We'll need to go get you some new

clothes?" he asked, glancing at the clock above the sink. "Can you be ready in thirty minutes?"

"Sure. I also need to collect a laptop and a remote access device from the Family Services Department in Rock Springs to enable me to continue working while we're away." She was worried about sounding demanding. "If this is all too much hassle, please go on without me. I can find somewhere to stay locally. I'll be fine."

Brent turned and leaned on the kitchen counter, his hands tucked behind his back. He and his deputies had decided to shun their uniforms in favor of civilian clothes, and Brent was wearing a sweatshirt and black cargo pants with a baseball cap folded into the front pocket.

"Carly, listen to me," he said firmly. "You won't be fine without somebody looking out for you. The photographs that were found in Odell's car make his intentions very clear. He wants to eliminate you." He grimaced as if realizing that his phrasing was too harsh. "At the very least, he wants to see you hurt. This campaign he's launched is not only about kidnapping Noah and Ruby but also making sure you suffer payback for taking them away from him in the first place." He walked toward her and touched her arm. "I know it's hard being stuck with me but it's in your best interest."

She took a deep breath and considered the alternative. She could rent a new apartment or stay in a hotel, and both ideas filled her with dread. Even if she purchased a firearm, she wouldn't have the confidence to use it. She'd never fired a gun in her life.

"I agree," she said, attempting to lighten the heavy mood that had descended by adding, "it *is* hard being stuck with you."

He laughed. "It's a good thing I have a thick skin. Let's go into Pinedale now and pick up the stuff you need. I'll send one of my deputies to collect your laptop and any other devices from Rock Springs. How does that sound?"

His kindness was a little overwhelming. "It sounds perfect. Is it safe to go out, do you think?"

"We'll be as careful as possible, but we have to take the risk unless you want my deputies to pick out your clothes. We stick together and never separate, and we won't stray from busy Pine Street. Got it?"

"Got it." She touched her still damp hair. "I'll just go shape my hair into a straw bale and we're good to go."

He laughed again. "Ruby really did mean it as a compliment. She loves everything about the petting zoo. I hope you're not hurt by what she said."

"Of course not." She shrugged it off. "I've been working with kids my whole life. Their honesty is one of the many reasons why I love them."

"For what it's worth, I think your hair is very pretty." He turned to busy himself with the dishwasher once more. "And you're beautiful."

The unexpected compliment caught her off guard but didn't succeed in making her feel good. Without another word, she headed for the stairs. Brent was no doubt trying to work his way into her affections, hoping he could speed up the adoption process with the use of flattery. Well, it wouldn't work. She wasn't that easily fooled.

Carly rifled through the racks with a false smile plastered across her face. These clothes weren't to her tastes at all, but Evan's Country Supplies was the only clothing store in town. She'd simply have to make do with pleated skirts, elasticated slacks and button-up blouses. Alternatively, she could choose rubber boots, waterproof pants and raincoats from the outdoors section.

Brent sidled up alongside her and spoke out of the corner of his mouth. "I think that Evan's clientele is generally a lot older than you. My mom adores it here, but this stuff probably isn't what you had in mind."

She didn't want to offend Evan, the store owner, who stood by the cash register, looking her way. She nodded a greeting at him and he came out from behind his counter.

"Having trouble making up your mind?" he said. "You can try items for size in our fitting room if you want."

"Um…no, thank you," she said, pushing hangers of cardigans along a rack. "I don't suppose you have any jeans and sweatpants, do you? I'm just looking for simple things."

"Actually, I had some new stock delivered a few months ago that didn't sell well, so I put it out back. I'll go get it."

He disappeared behind a curtain and returned with three boxes on a hand cart. Carly's heart surged with relief when he opened them up to reveal blue jeans, plain T-shirts, sweatpants and sweaters.

"My customers are on the traditional side," he said, pulling out items and holding them up. "My attempts to modernize them fell flat, I'm afraid."

"That's exactly what I'm looking for," she said, beginning to select T-shirts and sweat-shirts from the box. "This is perfect."

Carly chose a number of items plus some sneakers from the footwear section. As Evan rang up her purchases at the register, she slid some underwear onto the counter, thankful that Brent was busy keeping watch at the window.

"Are you and the sheriff taking a trip some-where?" Evan asked, placing her purchases into a couple of bags.

"We're not dating or anything," she said, probably sounding a little too horrified. "He's just helping me out after my apartment got burned up recently."

"You must be one of the apartment owners from Sycamore Street." He shook his head. "Terrible news about that fire." He punched the numbers into his charge card machine. "I'm glad the sheriff is giving you a helping hand." Leaning across the counter he added, "You two sure look good together even if you're not dating."

She gave him a forced smile as he handed over her bags. She hadn't yet introduced her-self to Pinedale, so most of the townsfolk wouldn't know that she was Brent's adoption caseworker and they certainly wouldn't be aware of the friction that existed between them as a result.

"Thank you, Evan," she said, turning and walking over to Brent, who was staring intently at a store across the street.

"What do you see?" she asked.

"I don't know. There are a couple of guys in the ice-cream parlor acting suspiciously. They keep looking over here as if they're waiting for us to leave."

Carly placed her bags on the carpet. "Is one of them Odell?"

"No, but we know he has accomplices. He might be lying low after almost getting caught last night and sending his friends to do his dirty work instead."

"What should we do?"

He picked up one of the bags and took her hand. "We leave."

Carly retrieved the other bag and allowed Brent to lead her out of the store, where his truck was parked at the curb. As Brent's old truck had been badly damaged the previous day, he'd organized an immediate replacement. But this new vehicle was plain and unmarked, as he didn't want to draw attention. With his eyes flicking to the ice-cream parlor across the street, he opened up the back door and placed Carly's bags on the seat.

"I think they're gone," he said. "I can't see them anymore."

This news came as a huge relief to Carly, as she desperately needed just a few more items. "Can we go to the drugstore real quick? I won't take long."

Brent checked the street in both directions. It was busy with people going about their business, but this obviously didn't reassure him.

"I'll stand guard on the sidewalk while you go inside," he said. "If you hear me call your name, drop everything and get out of there."

"Okay."

Brent's strong words caused a lump of fear to form in her throat and she tried to swallow it away as she headed inside the drugstore and picked up a basket. Making a speedy walk through the aisles, she selected the toiletries that she required and joined the line for the cashier. That's when she heard the gunshot that sent everybody scattering through the store, screaming and running for cover.

Then her name rang out across the chaos. Brent was calling for her.

FOUR

From her position crouched behind a magazine stand, Carly heard a series of pops as a gun discharged repeatedly. Between shots, she heard the sounds of screaming coming from customers who had taken cover on the floor between shelves rather than risk being shot while fleeing for the exit. She didn't know if Brent had managed to get inside as the shooting began. She didn't dare poke her head above the rack to take a look.

The shots finally ceased and Carly held her breath, waiting to see what would happen next. Should she try to make a run for it? Or was she safer remaining out of sight? She just couldn't make a decision. People whimpered all around her, clearly terrified.

Then a voice rang out. "I'm here for just one person. As long as she comes out, the rest of you will live."

The blood in Carly's veins turned to ice. He was talking about her.

"Where are you, Carly Engelman?" the man called. "Don't let these good people die. I'll shoot them one by one until I find you."

She pressed a hand hard over her mouth to prevent a sob escaping. If she revealed herself, she would be killed immediately, but if she remained hidden then several people could find themselves in the firing line because of her cowardice. Looking down at her shaking hands, still clutching her purse, she felt nothing but stone-cold terror.

A child's voice was the next thing she heard—a girl calling out for her mother. The sound was heartbreaking and gave the gunman a focus. The girl yelped and cried as she was clearly manhandled from her hiding position. The depraved man now had leverage.

"This little girl is the first to get a bullet," he said. "And I'm in a hurry, so I'll count to three."

He didn't need to begin his countdown because Carly jumped up in an instant. She saw the ski-masked gunman holding a girl of around eight years old by the hood of her jacket. The girl's mother stood nearby, pleading silently with him with outstretched hands, as he held his gun to her daughter's head.

They were the only people visible in the drugstore, but Carly knew that plenty of others were hiding, because she could hear their low cries and softly uttered prayers.

"I'm Carly Engelman," she said. "Let the child go. Please. You're scaring her."

Carly hated to see children in fear. It tore her up inside. Releasing kids from torment was one of the reasons she got out of bed in the morning. And she would sacrifice anything to save just one single child.

The man let go of the girl, who quickly darted into her mother's arms and wept with relief. Then the gun was aimed at Carly. She squeezed her eyes tightly closed and sent up a request to God, asking for every single life around her to be spared.

The shot came, a deafening sound that brought with it more screams of terror. She waited for the inevitable sting of pain, for her legs to give way and her body to hit the floor. But she remained standing. Opening her eyes, she saw the gunman lying on the ground, flat on his back, spread-eagled with his gun beside his lifeless hand. A well-placed shot to the chest had taken him down. Turning around, she saw Brent standing behind the cashier counter, maintaining the rigid pose that he must've used to take his shot. When it became apparent that the gunman was acting alone, he lowered his weapon and called out to the small crowd of hidden people.

"I'm Sheriff Brent Fox of Sublette County. The threat has been neutralized and you're all safe. The local police are en route. I'd like each of you to make your way to the front of the store and wait for the all-clear. Do not leave until you're directed to do so. Stay calm, folks, and just focus on following the sound of my voice. Everything is under control."

Carly watched Brent with a mixture of admiration and gratitude. The way he was taking charge of the situation and reassuring these anxious people was amazing. His authority was entirely natural, not forced or based on pretense. She had been trying so very hard not to like him, because she didn't want any personal feelings to muddy the waters surrounding the adoption decision. She needed to be thorough and tough, ensuring that no warning bells were overlooked. She had to remain detached.

But then he went and saved her life for the second time.

Brent wanted to go home. While he knew that Noah and Ruby were perfectly safe with his deputies, and a patrol car was keeping watch at the curbside, he hated to be separated from his children. Yet, a man had lost his life on Pine Street that day, and he understood that any death should be treated with reverence, no matter who it was. There were statements to give and eyewitness accounts to record, as well as security footage to preserve. The scene also had to be made secure for the police photographers and forensics team to document crucial evidence. He couldn't leave until the analysis had been completed, and this procedure had run into several hours already.

"I thought you could use a pick-me-up," he said, handing Carly a coffee from the shop across the street. "It has an extra shot of espresso."

"Thanks."

She took the paper cup and curled her hands around it. She appeared to have stopped shaking, but her pallor was still showing signs of shock. Her skin was flawless, but was without color, and she had been staring into space while the police went about their business. She was miles away.

He sat next to her on the sidewalk bench outside the drugstore. "You okay?"

"I think so. I've never seen a dead person before, so it'll take a while to get the image out of my head."

"I understand." In his job, Brent was used to seeing lifeless bodies so it didn't faze him so much. "I'm sorry you had to go through this ordeal. For what it's worth, I thought you were a superhero today. I've seen plenty of people face dangerous situations and none of them stepped up like you did."

She appeared confused. "What do you mean?"

"The way you offered yourself in exchange for the girl's life was amazing. Trust me, most people would've stayed hidden, but you jumped up without a second's thought." He looked into her eyes, to make sure she knew how strongly he felt. "You should be proud of yourself. Not everybody is as brave as you."

She took a sip of coffee and gazed at the ground. "I can't stand to see a child crying out for help. I'd do anything to stop them being hurt, even if it means putting myself in harm's way." He saw moisture gather in her eyes. "It's beyond my comprehension how an adult can deliberately place a child in danger. We're meant to be their guardians and protectors."

"I agree entirely."

The fact that Carly had been prepared to sacrifice herself to save the child had floored Brent. And wowed him. He knew this straight-talking child protection officer was dedicated, but he'd had no idea how much. Seeing her face the barrel of a gun with such courage and dignity had flipped a switch in him. While she was still the main obstacle in his adoption process, she had now also become somebody he wanted to know better. Carly was the kind of honorable woman he had always been drawn to. She possessed an integrity that spoke to him on a deep level.

"I know you said that you and God aren't on speaking terms," he said. "But you clearly have an internal strength that comes from Him."

She thought about this for a while. "Maybe. I certainly felt Him standing with me when I thought I was going to die. I knew He would take care of me whatever happened."

He was glad to hear this positive affirmation of her faith. "Sometimes it takes an experience like this to teach us how to submit to God's will."

She smiled and he instinctively reached for her hand, sandwiching it between his own. She seemed to appreciate the gesture, letting out a gentle sigh and closing her eyes as if allowing the stress of the morning to melt away.

"I haven't thanked you for saving me," she

said. "Again. I'm really grateful for what you did."

"You actually helped me a lot by standing up and showing yourself. It caused the gunman to stop moving and that allowed me to take a sure shot."

When the shooting had first started, Brent had managed to sneak inside the store among the chaos. He had then hidden himself behind the counter to wait for the gunman to come into view. Randomly firing his gun in a store would've been disastrous so he'd wanted to be sure of an accurate aim. He'd had no idea where Carly was hiding, and he couldn't risk calling her name. The simple act of her revealing her hiding spot had given him the perfect opportunity, and the gunman had been taken by surprise to see Brent pop up from the counter. Carly wasn't aware of it, but they'd worked as a team.

"Do we know who the guy is?" she asked. "I didn't recognize the voice."

"One of the police officers thinks he recognizes his face. He's a hitman for hire who's been involved in some turf war incidents across the state over the years. He's usually paid to break legs or leave bruises, but it looks like he progressed to taking money to commit murder."

He saw her shiver, so he scooted closer and placed an arm around her shoulder. He probably shouldn't get this close, but she needed the comfort and reassurance. And he wanted to provide it.

"There were two of them," she said quietly. "Do you remember? You saw two suspicious men in the ice-cream parlor while we were shopping. If one of them got in through the back door of the drugstore, that means the other one could still be here." She looked around the vicinity with darting eyes. "Do you think he's watching us right now?"

"Unlikely. The entire area is crawling with law enforcement. But I think it's a good idea if we leave and head to our safe house as soon as possible. I'll go speak to the police chief and ask if he needs anything more from us." He stood up. "Stay put and I'll be right back."

She smiled weakly. "It's not like I have anywhere else to be. I'm in your hands now."

He turned and headed to the throng of officers outside the drugstore. To be reminded that Carly was in his hands was confusing. He was conflicted. On the one hand, he wanted to keep her close and safe. On the other hand, he wanted to reject her for being a thorn in his side and dragging out the adoption case.

He just didn't know what to feel anymore.

* * *

The peace and tranquility of the lakeside cabin took Carly's breath away. Fremont Lake was only a few miles from Pinedale, so it had taken no time at all to reach, but it felt like a different world. Brent had been offered the use of a large and remote cabin at the base of the Wind River Mountains, hidden in the woods. The owner of the lodge was a court judge and friend who had gotten wind of Brent's situation and stepped in to assist. Brent had kept the location a secret from Carly and the children until they arrived late in the afternoon, just as the sky was turning a deep orange on the rugged peaks of the mountain range.

She explored the place, looking into every room, while the children charged around excitedly, squealing with delight. To them, this was an unexpected vacation and they didn't question why it included two sheriff's deputies and their adoption caseworker. Carly had been pleased to find her laptop and electronic devices already at the cabin, having been collected from Rock Springs and delivered there by one of Brent's trusted deputies. This would allow her to continue her important work, as well as progressing with Brent's adoption case.

She knew she would have to face this decision sooner or later. These children needed stability. They deserved a permanent family. And Brent was not only a good father, but he was a strong protector. He would always guarantee their happiness and safety, giving them an upbringing that would ensure they turned into emotionally healthy adults.

A vision forced itself into her mind and she gripped the doorframe of the games room as she passed by. In her mind, Brent was standing in front of the children with a gun pointed at Ruby's head.

"No," she said out loud. "No."

"Don't you like it?" Brent said from the end of the hallway. "Is it too remote for you?"

She shook away the horrible image. "I love the place. It's beautiful. I was thinking about something else, that's all. Something to do with work."

"You looked really distressed for a moment." He walked toward her. "Do you want to talk about it?"

"No!" She realized she'd said this too loudly and too harshly. "No, thank you. I'm okay."

He eyed her with what looked like suspicion, as if he could see she was lying. Brent seemed to be able to see right through her pretense. She wasn't okay. She hadn't been okay since switching on the television five months ago to discover that Oliver Dowd, a well-respected doctor and adoptive father, had killed his family before turning the gun on himself. The news had shaken her to the core, forcing her to confront the very real possibility that she was to blame for this tragedy. She had placed Laurie in his care. Had the addition of a child in his family somehow caused a change in his mental state? Had she moved too fast? She had subsequently pored over the adoption documentation, seeking answers to numerous questions, but it didn't help. It only made things worse. There were no easy answers.

"Listen," Brent said, pulling a small gun from the pocket of his jacket. "I wanted you to have Tamsin's old gun for protection. I know you're not familiar with weapons, so I'd be happy to give you a crash course outside. Of course, we won't actually fire any shots, but I can show you how it works."

She didn't like this idea at all. "I'm not sure, Brent. I don't like guns."

"I don't especially like guns either, but I understand that they're necessary in defending innocent people. Clarence Odell is a highly dangerous individual and he's targeted you for revenge and my children for kidnapping. Please just think about keeping hold of this for emergencies."

She relented because he made a lot of sense. "Okay. I'll think about it."

He slid the gun back into his pocket. "You know Odell's character far better than I do, so I was wondering if you had any ideas about what he might do next, or where he might go. He needs to be caught and the police have no leads right now."

"I'm sorry but I don't know enough about his associates to pinpoint where he might be staying," she said. "After he lost the custody case, I figured that he'd finally run out of money and would disappear. He's never been a big earner so somebody must be helping him financially. I don't know how much a hitman costs but I'm sure it's more than Odell can afford. He's not a smart man, so I think somebody is bankrolling him."

"Who?"

"I have no idea."

Brent sighed. The anxiety and stress were showing on his face, as creases seemed to be permanently etched into his forehead. He was clearly desperate to catch Odell and return to a normal life, but that was currently out of reach.

"I try really hard not to hate people, but I'm failing when it comes to Clarence Odell," he said, clenching his fists at his side. "I just hate the guy with every cell in my body."

"That's because he's a despicable man. When he petitioned for custody of Noah and Ruby, everybody in the courtroom saw his true personality, even his own lawyer. He was belligerent and argumentative, lying through his teeth about being the main caregiver for the children when he'd spent most of his time on the street or fleeing from the cops. It was obvious that he was a danger to the children, so don't feel bad about resenting Odell. He's earned every bit of your hatred."

Brent nodded slowly, taking his time to respond. "I guess it's often pretty easy to see which parents should be stopped from raising their kids, huh?"

This was a no-brainer. "Absolutely."

"If you can tell which parents are the bad ones, then that allows you to identify the good ones, right?"

She could see where he was leading her. And she didn't like it, because she could feel herself being backed into a corner.

"It's not always obvious," she said. "Sometimes when somebody says all the right things and looks good on paper, they can still be dangerous. That's why child protection officers take no chances. We have to be thorough."

"And that's what you're doing with my case? Being thorough."

The way he said these words sounded like he was mocking her and she adopted a defiant tone in response. "Yes. Do you have a problem with that?"

"It doesn't matter what I think. You're the one holding all the power."

She swallowed away a sense of hurt. He was implying that she was wielding her authority with spite, and that wasn't true at all.

"My job is incredibly difficult, Brent," she said coolly. "It isn't always apparent who represents a danger to children, and if prospective parents have to wait a little longer while I make additional checks then it's worth it in the end."

He stared at her, shaking his head. "You know me." He took her hand and repeated the words, slower this time. "You. Know. Me. Look into my eyes and tell me that I represent a danger to my children."

She looked into his face and saw the deep brown rings around his hazel irises. His eyes were soft and warm, full of compassion and kindness. She could see no malice in him at all. What was more, she was mesmerized by him. The way he held her gaze with such intensity was intoxicating, and she momentarily forgot the subject of their conversation.

"I want to be the best father I can be," he said, snapping her out of her daydream.

She took a sudden step backward, jolted by these words. Oliver Dowd had said the exact same thing: *I want to be the best father I can be.* He had pulled the wool over her eyes, hiding his dark and terrifying intentions. She had lapped up his promises without question.

"I appreciate your patience while the adoption process moves forward." The only way she could continue this discussion was with overt formality. "I'll keep you regularly updated as we make progress."

"Hey, where did you go?" He was continuing to hold her gaze. "Whenever I get too close, you pull down the shutters and check out. What's going on with you? We're friends now, so talk to me."

"We're not friends, Mr. Fox. I'm your adoption caseworker and you're my client. Let's not get ahead of ourselves."

"Okay, Ms. Engelman, have it your way. But I want you to remember that I love my kids and they will never come to harm while they're with me."

With a huge effort, Carly maintained a calm demeanor, despite wanting to let out a scream of frustration. Brent was right. She *did* know him. And he was a good man. Her head told her so. Yet, when she closed her eyes, the vision of him holding a gun to Ruby's head continued to taunt her. She would rather risk Brent hating her forever than losing another child to her stupidity.

Carly appeared to be responding well under Brent's tutoring, even allowing him to place himself behind her and position the gun correctly. She had agreed to learn how to use Tamsin's old mini revolver, accepting that it might prove to be a crucial means of defense. He had already given her a long and detailed description of how the weapon worked and the importance of complying with common sense safety measures.

"Always be aware of your target and what surrounds it," he said, guiding the sight to line up with the piece of paper he had pinned to a tree trunk as a marker. "Only shoot when you're certain of hitting your intended target rather than anybody else nearby. Got it?"

"Got it."

Brent brought his face down to align with hers, so that their cheeks were touching. His posture was akin to hugging her from behind and the physical closeness was unsettling for him. He didn't want to overstep his boundaries, but it was important that Carly learned how to aim correctly. He also didn't want to enjoy being close to her, but he was fighting a losing battle on that front. Something about her stirred him emotionally. Maybe it was the vulnerability that she tried hard to hide. Or her feistiness. Or the way she tucked her hair behind her ears repeatedly when she was nervous. Most likely it was a mixture of all these things, and more besides. After Tamsin died, Brent hadn't planned on looking at another woman in this way for a very long time. But life clearly had other ideas, because Carly was giving him chills that he had not expected.

"You'll feel a recoil in your hands and arms after pulling the trigger," he said. "That's why it's important to maintain a good posture and be well-balanced on your feet." He took one hand off the revolver and squeezed her shoulder. "You're tensing up, and that will mess with your aim in a real-life situation. Relax your muscles."

She lowered the weapon and dropped her head. "This is so hard, Brent. Guns scare me."

He gathered her into his arms and held her close. She responded to his comforting gesture by burying her face in his sweatshirt and letting out a long breath that permeated through the thick, cotton fabric and onto his chest. Brent totally understood why she felt this way about guns. They were capable of inflicting terrible damage. Yet, they were also a useful tool in saving lives. It depended on whose hands they rested in.

At least she had reverted to calling him Brent again, instead of Mr. Fox. Their earlier disagreement was still lingering, and neither had spoken about it since. Carly had lashed out when telling him that they weren't friends, and he tried not to be hurt by it. Her reaction had been one of defensiveness because he had gotten too close to something she preferred remained hidden. And he wanted to know what it was.

"You're doing great," he said. "I can see this is hard for you." He wondered if there was a deeper cause for her discomfort. "Is there a reason why you feel so strongly about firearms? Did something happen to make you afraid?"

He felt her tensing up again, but she remained pressed against his torso. Turning her face to the side, she started talking.

"You've been a sheriff for a long time, right?"

"More than ten years."

"You must've dealt with a lot of shootings."

"Yes."

"Did you ever come across a person who shot somebody they loved?"

He thought about this for a while, wondering what had prompted her to ask such a question. Was she concerned about shooting one of the children by mistake?

"Tragic accidents sometimes happen," he said. "That's why we're taking time to go through these safety procedures, to make sure you know exactly what to do."

She pulled away from him, the gun still hanging at her side, and stepped away. The leaves and twigs of the forest crunched under her sneaker and she bent down to place the gun at her feet, as if she no longer wanted the weight of it in her hand.

"No," she said. "I mean on purpose. Have you ever known a person who shot somebody they love on purpose?"

Again, he took a while to consider her question. "It's happened a few times during my career. It usually occurs when there's a history of family violence or domestic abuse. We always advise people who are threatened with gun violence to leave the home immediately, but unfortunately, they often stay because they don't think their loved one will go through with it."

She seemed to be listening carefully to his words. "Is there a way of knowing who might be at risk of committing this type of offense? Is there some kind of test that would identify a potential shooter?"

"There are warning signs sometimes, but other times it can come out of the blue and…"

She didn't let him finish. "What are the warning signs?"

"A history of drug and alcohol abuse, a volatile personality, anger issues, previous domestic violence claims or convictions, displaying a disregard for gun safety measures. These are all red flags when it comes to gun ownership."

"Are there any other warning signs? Ones that might be more subtle?"

"Are you talking about a specific person here, Carly?" he asked. "Because if there's something you need to talk about, I'm a very good listener. And I can give you my professional opinion if you want it."

She shook her head. "I was just talking generally." She looked down at the gun nestled in the leaves. "This weapon can end a person's life in a matter of seconds, so I wanted to know how to spot someone who would misuse it."

It was obvious she wasn't telling him the whole story, but he didn't press her for details. She might confide in him at some point, but now was not the time.

"Sometimes there is no way of knowing who will misuse a gun," he said truthfully. "Certain individuals in society will commit random acts of violence entirely without warning. It's a sad part of life that we can't control."

"So you're saying that nobody can ever truly be trusted. Because if there's no way of knowing who will flip out, then everybody is a potential risk." She looked him dead straight in the eye. "Even you."

"If you assume that every person you meet is dangerous, then you'll end up trusting no one at all." He picked up the gun. "And that's no way to live."

She took the gun from his hand, apparently ready to restart their lesson.

"I'm responsible for the lives of children," she said. "I have to assume that every person is dangerous until I'm certain of their intentions."

Her face was close to breaking and he sensed the well of pain that she'd bottled up inside. Something awful had happened to make her this cautious. He wished she would confide in him, so that he could help her deal with the torment. But if she refused to give him details then he would have no choice other than to continue pressing her for the completion of the adoption. If that meant more arguments and bitterness, so be it.

His children belonged with him. Carly's distrustful attitude would not derail the process.

FIVE

Noah stood in the living room of the cabin with his hands on his hips, and his face was set in an expression of annoyance.

"Why can't we go outside?" he whined to Brent. "You went outside with Carly yesterday. I saw you go into the woods."

"That was different," Brent replied. "We had something important to do yesterday."

"Like holding hands?" Ruby piped up from the corner of the room where she was sitting with her doll, while pretending the bookcase was a dollhouse. "Or kissing? That's what grown-ups do when they go off by themselves. A boy in school told me."

"No," Brent said as he flicked his eyes to Carly, who was perched on the arm of the sofa next to him. She was covering a smile with her hand. "We were not holding hands or kissing." He turned toward his foster daughter. "Don't believe everything that boys in school tell you, Ruby. They aren't always right."

"What *were* you doing?" Noah asked, now intrigued. "You were gone a long time."

"We were looking for shells," Carly interjected quickly. "It's for a project I'm doing."

Brent turned to her and mouthed the word *shells* with a bemused expression. Noah was also similarly confused.

"But we're in a forest," he said. "Shells are beach things."

Carly threw her hands up in the air dramatically. "Well, that must be why we didn't find any. I guess I'll have to go look on a beach instead." She stood and walked to Noah, before bending down on one knee to look directly at him. "You're smart to know facts like this. I wish I'd asked you about shells before going into the forest. I'd have saved myself a lot of time and effort."

"I know a lot about the ocean," Noah said with pride, instantly responding to the positive praise. "I can tell you all about whales and dolphins and stingrays. I learned it from my favorite book."

"That's great," Carly said with a big smile. "Do you have the book with you?"

"Yeah." He hopped from one foot to the

other, obviously eager to show her. "It's in my room."

"I saw some crafting supplies in a cabinet in the hallway." She had clearly formulated a plan. "I think we should go get your book and make a collage of all the things that live in the ocean. That would be fun, right?"

Ruby jumped up. "Can I come too?"

"Of course. You can make the seahorses."

Brent sat back in his chair, admiring how Carly had masterfully turned this whole situation around. Noah had been bored and antsy, surrounded by trees and nature but being unable to go outdoors. Brent really didn't want to take any chances with their safety. Even though he felt safe and secure in their secluded cabin, he couldn't be certain that Odell wouldn't discover their hiding spot. He had told the children that the land around the cabin was private, and they weren't allowed to tread on it. It was a pretty flimsy excuse, but it was the best he could come up with. They had bounced back well after Odell's attempt to kidnap them, and he avoided mentioning it at all costs. He didn't want them to live in fear.

"You're a natural with kids," he said to Carly, taking a chance on throwing her a wink, which she returned with a smile as she passed. "I'll come join you as soon as I've had a catch-up with Liam. He's got some news to report."

"No problem. I'll be in the dining room, probably all sticky with glue."

He watched the three of them leave the room, with Carly holding each child by the hand. Noah and Ruby had quickly developed a real affection for her. They'd interacted with her previously as part of the adoption process but being at the cabin had changed the way they saw her. She was no longer somebody official, like a teacher, but a friend who played with them, read them books and cracked stupid jokes. The children brought out a completely different side to Carly, and he liked the change in her. She was often defensive and difficult when dealing with him but with the children she was goofy and happy. It was as though they made her forget the mysterious shadow that lingered over her. They broke through her hard shell in a way that he could only dream of.

He wondered why she didn't have children of her own. She would make a great mom. But he didn't know her situation. He knew better than anybody that the decision to have children wasn't always one that could be made easily. He and Tamsin had discussed it at length, going through all the options before deciding on fostering and adoption. It was the best decision they'd ever made, and if Carly would only move forward with the process, he'd be named as their legal father on their birth certificate. It couldn't come a moment too soon for him.

"Hey, boss, you ready for our chat?" Liam entered the room and sat on the couch opposite. "Amir is keeping watch out front."

"Sure. What have you got, Liam? Please tell me it's good news rather than bad."

"It's a little of both. The police took a look at the security footage at the ice-cream parlor in Pinedale, and it captured the two suspects who were loitering there yesterday. One of them was Wayne Kendrick, who ended up dead on the floor of the drugstore. The other was a man named Lamar Ryland, who was arrested last night after a traffic stop on the interstate just outside Cheyenne. He's in custody right now and he's singing like a canary."

Brent sat up straight. "This is great news, right? It means we'll have more information to track down Odell."

"Actually, it's more complicated than it seems. Kendrick and Ryland are hired hitmen from Cheyenne. They've been working as a pair for a couple years, specializing in beatings and torture. They've been wanted by the police for more than twelve months, but they've eluded the authorities until now. Ryland says that this is the first time they've agreed to carry out a murder. He was standing guard at the back entrance to the drugstore while Kendrick went inside to search for Carly. When his partner got taken down, Lamar fled the scene and tried to make it back to Cheyenne."

"What's complicated about this?" Brent asked. "It all sounds straightforward to me."

"They were both paid ten thousand dollars up front for the hit, with a promise of another fifteen thousand each once the job was done."

Brent quickly did the math. "That's fifty grand."

"Yep. I've done a little digging on Clarence Odell and he's not a man who could lay his hands on that kind of money. He's a two-bit drug dealer and a petty thief who's managed to stay out of prison by the skin of his teeth. He's been fined a whole bunch of times by the courts and he's always struggled to come up with the money. This guy doesn't have fifty dollars to his name, let alone fifty grand."

Brent instantly remembered what Carly had said about Odell possibly being bankrolled. Was somebody supplying him with unlimited funds to further his vendetta? Who would have a vested interest in helping Odell terminate Carly? Or assist him in kidnapping Noah and Ruby?

"How were Kendrick and Ryland paid? Did Odell hire them?"

"The initial contact came from Odell but Ryland said that he and Kendrick were paid in cash via an anonymous drop outside a disused warehouse in Cheyenne. He said there were two expensive SUVs parked outside, watching their every move. The money was handed over by a man in a clown mask who warned them that they'd face repercussions if they messed up. Ryland believes the man who hired them is a big-time gangster, not little league like Odell."

Brent thought of the clown masks worn by Odell and his accomplices. He had assumed this was Odell's idea, but they could've been supplied by somebody else, by the person who was pulling the strings.

"Do we have any leads on who might've paid Kendrick and Lamar? Any security footage of the SUVs heading to or from the warehouse?"

Liam shook his head. "They probably picked that spot because it was so quiet, with no cameras anywhere nearby. The Cheyenne police have nothing so far, but it seems likely that the gang who handed over the money is a successful one, with a lot of criminal contacts and influence. Ryland is terrified that he'll be killed for failing to carry out the hit successfully. He wants to enter witness protection in return for his cooperation."

Brent ran a hand down his face and pulled at the strands of his beard. Liam had been correct in saying that this news was complicated. While it gave them a lot of information, it threw up more questions than it answered.

"Did Ryland know anything about the plan to kidnap Noah and Ruby?"

"No. He says he was hired solely to terminate Carly, and he was told nothing about a kidnapping plot. For what it's worth, the officers who interviewed him said they believed everything he said. He's really scared. He needs the police's protection right now, so I don't think he'd lie."

"If Odell has a powerful accomplice, then he could have a far greater reach than I originally thought. Let's be hypervigilant for anything that might seem suspicious." He stood up. "But right now, I have a more important duty to carry out."

"Are you going to do some research?"

"No. I'll be making whales and dolphins out of tissue paper. For the next couple hours, I'll be pretending that everything is just fine."

Carly peeled glue residue from her hands while logging into her work email. She had spent the morning making a huge ocean collage with Noah, Ruby and, surprisingly, Brent. She had initially been awkward with him when he joined them at the table. Their relationship was still a little frosty at times, largely because he continued to press her for reasons why the adoption process was taking so long. She had also seemed to pique his interest by asking how to spot red flags in gun owners. He had mentioned it a couple times since, trying to get her to elaborate on why she wanted to know. She regretted asking those questions, because it did nothing to alleviate her fears. According to Brent, there was no way of telling who might commit random acts of violence. And that just wasn't a good enough explanation. There must be a way to know. There simply had to be signs she had missed in Oliver Dowd.

She cast her mind back while waiting for her email to load on her laptop. Oliver Dowd had been a keen runner and was super fit and active. He earned good money, owned a beautiful home and appeared to love his wife greatly. There was one time when he snapped at her when her cell phone rang in the middle of their adoption meeting, but Carly hadn't thought much of it at the time. She'd put it down to Mr. Dowd's nerves and the fact he'd wanted no distractions, but maybe she should've spoken to Mrs. Dowd afterward. That one offhand comment could've been a sign of worse things at home. She should have taken more care.

A series of reminders pinged onto the screen in front of her, telling her of documentation that she had to submit and meetings to attend. She slapped a hand to her forehead, reading the prompts. In all the drama she had forgotten about an important family court hearing she was due to attend in Cheyenne the following day. There was no way she could miss it. She was overseeing a court battle between a divorcing couple, in which Child Protective Services was supporting the mother, Zoe Buchannan.

Zoe had applied for sole custody of her ten-month-old baby son, Jordan, but her husband, Kendall, was petitioning for visitation rights. Kendall Buchannan was a well-known criminal in Cheyenne, involved in all kinds of organized crime, and he was currently awaiting trial for murder. Zoe had agreed to be a witness for the prosecution and was certain that if Kendall were awarded visitation rights, he would steal her child and disappear. Wyoming Family Services had sided with the mother and it was Carly's job to persuade the judge to terminate the rights of the father. Kendall Buchannan reminded her of Clarence Odell in many ways. Both men were abusive and dangerous, and saw their children as possessions. The simple fact was that children should always be removed from those who would cause them harm.

"You look stressed. What's up?"

Brent was standing in the doorway of her makeshift office, which was really a small gym containing an exercise bike and treadmill. A table and chair had been placed in the corner, and Brent had set up an organized workspace with all the things she might need, including a printer. She had been touched by his consideration.

"I have to go to Cheyenne tomorrow for an important court case. Do you think you could ask Amir or Liam to take me?"

He came into the room and leaned against the treadmill. Wearing khaki cargo pants and a fitted black T-shirt, he looked a little like a soldier in uniform. She didn't know whether he worked out, but something had given him a honed physique. She guessed that somebody as busy as Brent must give himself a workout just with his daily activities.

"If it's okay with you, I'd like to accompany you," he replied. "I know the roads between here and Cheyenne better than anyone. If we run into any trouble, I can take us off the interstate and use alternate routes."

She would much rather sit in a car with Amir or Liam, and she obviously didn't do a good job of hiding her disappointment.

"Look," he said, walking across the carpet to perch on the edge of the table. "I know we have our ups and downs, but I promise that I'll always put your safety at the top of my list of priorities. Just because I have a problem with the amount of time you're taking to complete the adoption process doesn't mean I have a problem taking care of you."

"Thank you." Mention of the adoption reminded her of something. "Actually, I have a questionnaire for you to complete to support your adoption application." She navigated through the folders on her laptop screen until she found the right one. "I'll just print it so you can take a look."

The printer whirred to life and rolled out a single piece of paper, which Brent picked up and began to read while standing next to her. She saw his eyebrows wrinkle and his lips pinch.

"Is this an official questionnaire from Wyoming Family Services?" he asked. "I wasn't expecting to receive something like this."

"It's something I devised myself. Child protection officers are given a lot of leeway in how they conduct their work in the department, so we're allowed to ask questions that aren't routine." She smiled in order to diffuse the tension that had built up. "I'm just dotting all the i's and crossing all the t's."

He began to read out loud some of the questions she had created. "How many guns are in your home? Where are they kept? Who has access to them?" He looked at her with incredulity. "Are you seriously questioning my attitude toward gun safety? I'm an expert in firearms, Carly. I even give training to various organizations on how to use guns responsibly." He shook his head. "This has got to be a joke?"

"No joke." She had expected this reaction from him and was prepared for the backlash. "If you want me to place two children in your home on a permanent basis then you need to reassure me that they won't become victims of a shooting."

He blinked fast, as if a hundred thoughts were swirling around his head at that moment.

"Children are at risk from all kinds of things," he said, listing them one by one on his hand. "Road traffic accidents, infections, congenital diseases, falling from windows. There are probably hundreds of ways that a child can come to harm. Why are you so obsessed with this one particular risk?"

"Because in my opinion, it's the most serious one."

Deep down, she knew that Brent was right. Children faced many risks in life, but the danger presented by guns weighed on her mind constantly. She couldn't overcome the fear that sat in the pit of her belly all the time, giving her constant twinges to remind her of the worst that can happen. After losing Laurie so tragically, Carly had requested a hiatus from overseeing adoptions, and she had been handed no new cases since. But Brent's case predated Laurie's murder, so she had to see it through. The power that she held regarding the approval of adoptions was almost too much to bear now. Her confidence in her abilities had been shattered. She was broken.

"Why are you asking me if I've ever shot a person?" he asked, still scanning the list of questions. "I've been a law enforcement officer for twenty years. It stands to reason that I've been required to shoot a suspect on occasion. Why would this have any relevance to my application to adopt Noah and Ruby?"

"Have you shot a lot of people?" she asked. "It sounds like you might have."

His nostrils flared. "Are you calling me trigger-happy?"

She stared at him, her whole body compelling her to ask the question that would surely anger Brent even more. "*Are* you trigger-happy?"

He crumpled up the paper and tossed it aside. "This is a farce. I just can't understand you, Carly. You're an amazing woman. You're thoughtful and courageous, and the way you step up every day to protect children just blows me away. Sometimes, I even find myself wanting to be close to you because I admire you in so many ways. But then you do something like this."

"Like what?"

"Like making me jump through pointless hoops and answer stupid questions that have no bearing on my ability to be a good father. Especially when you know my job will require me to answer these questions in a way that could be misinterpreted." He took a deep breath, possibly trying to calm himself. "It's petty."

She balked. "Petty? You think that making sure your home environment is suitable for children is petty?"

"You know that law enforcement officers have children. The way you've crafted your questionnaire would make them seem reckless and bias Family Services against them." He raised his voice. "What exactly are you afraid of?"

The answer was out of her mouth before she could stop it. "I'm afraid of what you might do once the kids are officially yours."

"Once those kids are officially mine, I plan on loving them for the rest of my days, giving thanks to God for bringing them into my life. I guess you'll need to work overtime to protect them from that unimaginable horror, right?"

She was stunned into silence by his passionate words and their eyes locked for a few seconds. Brent's expression was loaded with a direct challenge, waiting for her to bounce the ball back into his court once more. Instead of continuing the argument, she spoke quietly.

"I'll email you the schedule for tomorrow. We'll have to leave pretty early and I'll organize a security pass so you can enter the courthouse if you choose, but you might want to wait in the car with the radio on. Family hearings can drag on, so I recommend taking something to occupy yourself. It might be a long day."

He sighed, nodded curtly and stalked from the room.

Brent was tired and sore behind the wheel of his truck on the interstate. He hadn't slept well and had risen frequently to check that everything was okay in the cabin. Liam and Amir had agreed to give him a night off guard duty in order to allow him a long sleep before the five-hour journey to Cheyenne in the morning. But he had been restless, tossing and turning while mulling over his heated conversation with Carly. There was something she wasn't telling him, and it was driving him crazy. More to the point, *she* was driving him crazy. Every time he closed his eyes, he saw her face, with her pale green eyes surrounded by waves of blond hair. He was growing increasingly attracted to her and he wanted it to stop, because she was the one person in his life with the power to crush his hopes and dreams. He had assumed up until this point that the legalities regarding the adoption were mere formalities. It had never crossed his mind that he might be rejected.

But now he was worried. Carly's behavior had given him cause for concern. The latest questionnaire that he was meant to complete had blindsided him. It was as if she was finding problems where none existed. His job meant that he kept a firearm in the home, just like plenty of other responsible people. She was clearly concerned about the weapon being used against the children, which was a risk that he mitigated. It was stored securely in a cabinet that only he could access. Accidents happened when people let their standards slip, and Brent was never complacent.

Unless she was concerned that he would harm them on purpose. Her comment about what might happen after the adoption was finalized had struck him as strange, implying that once Brent was Noah and Ruby's legal father, he could become a threat to them somehow. He had been offended by the remarks but also intrigued by them. Why had she said this? During the night he had decided he would try to get inside her head, to understand her driving force. At the same time, he would also have to fight his attraction to her. Pursuing a relationship with his adoption caseworker was the worst idea in the world.

Pulling into the parking lot of the Laramie County Courthouse of Cheyenne, he quickly scanned the area for signs of anything suspicious. He looked up at the huge redbrick building, with its imposing columns around the entrance, and decided that he would remain with the vehicle, where he could easily watch people entering and leaving. He gently tapped Carly on the shoulder.

"Hey, sleepyhead," he said. "Time to wake up. We're here."

She roused herself and rubbed at her temple. "Did I fall asleep?"

"Yeah. You went out like a light just after we set off."

"I'm sorry that I didn't keep you company." Her voice was groggy. "I didn't sleep well, so I guess I was tired." She glanced at him. "I couldn't stop thinking about the last time we spoke. I realized that I probably upset you with my questions."

He waited for the apology. It didn't come.

"Anyway," she said. "I hope we can move past it and focus on what's important."

"Sure we can."

He reached into his jacket pocket and pulled out a piece of paper. It was a little tatty after being crumpled and tossed on the floor, but he had tried to smooth out the creases as best he could. He had filled out each and every question, giving as much detail as he could.

"Here's your questionnaire," he said, handing it to her. "That should give you all the information you need."

She took it from him and slotted it into her briefcase. "Thank you."

He angled his body toward hers. "Every single time you place an obstacle in my path, I will overcome it, because I would crawl over hot coals for Noah and Ruby. If you want me to jump through pointless hoops, then I'll do it. I'll do whatever it takes to prove that I'm a worthy father."

"Okay," she said. "Duly noted."

He opened his car door and planted a foot on the concrete, ready to walk her to the entrance. He was determined to also do whatever it took to protect Carly. She may be a thorn in his side, but she was in the crosshairs of a deranged man with a grudge. And Brent would have to be her first line of defense.

Carly was exhausted after her court session. Both Zoe and Kendall Buchannan had been present, creating an atmosphere that could've been cut with a knife. Kendall had been wearing the electronic ankle tag that had been fitted as part of his bail conditions, and there was a heavy police presence to prevent him making any threats toward his wife. Zoe had clearly been anxious and afraid, unwilling to look at her husband as he stared at her in an attempt to be intimidating.

Just as she had done in the Clarence Odell custody hearing, Carly had argued passionately for a denial of visitation rights for Kendall Buchannan. This big-time gangster had a litany of offenses in his past, including committing acts of domestic violence against Zoe. He was not a safe parent for little Jordan to be around. The judge had ended the hearing by asking Carly to prepare a report for submission to the court, after which a final ruling would be made. It was a good sign, as the judge seemed to be sympathetic to Zoe's plight.

Now that Carly was back in the car, she was pleased it was all over.

From his position in the driver's seat, Brent looked across at her with raised eyebrows. "If that smile on your face is anything to go by, you had a good day in court."

"I did. I think I'll get the outcome I want."

"I'm guessing you always get the outcome you want."

She wasn't sure if this was a barb and decided to ignore it. Her relationship with Brent was becoming difficult, as he grew ever more frustrated with her. She wished she could loosen up, but it was beyond her control. Sometimes, the desire to tell him about Laurie's adoption and subsequent murder was overwhelming. She imagined the way he might comfort and reassure her. She could imagine it so well that she could almost feel his arms around her shoulders, holding her close. He just might make her feel unburdened.

But he also might blame her. After all, it *was* her fault.

"I don't know about you but I'm starving," Brent said after a minute's silence. "There's a diner just off the main road up ahead. Could you stand to spend an hour with me while having a meal?"

He made it sound as though she despised him, but that couldn't be further from the truth. She was beginning to like him a lot, and the thought of having dinner with him caused butterflies to swirl.

"I'd like that," she said.

He turned onto a quiet road, following a sign for the Mountain Retreat Diner. Carly leaned against the headrest, taking in the greenery around them. This was the first time in many months that she had felt anything close to peace. Yet, it wasn't to last, because Brent suddenly put his foot on the gas and flicked his eyes between the rearview mirror and the road ahead.

"Uh-oh," he said ominously. "There's a car on our tail. We need to get back on the interstate quickly."

Just as she turned her head to look at the threat, the rear end of the truck was smashed with such force that they veered onto the grassy shoulder and spun out of control.

SIX

The car rotated repeatedly, as Brent fought to control the skid and get them back onto the asphalt. The scenery outside rushed past the windows in a blur of green. Carly screamed and gripped the dash with her fingers, while Brent sent up a prayer, not only for him and Carly, but for his children, who had been safe when he checked just an hour ago but could be in a very different situation now.

Finally, his red pickup came to a stop on the grass by the side of the road, facing a forest a few yards ahead. The SUV was right behind them, revving its engine and preparing for another strike. Flooring the gas pedal, Brent took the only exit route available: through the trees. Bouncing on the uneven ground, he entered the darkness of the woods, weaving his way between the thick trunks, occasionally sideswiping the truck's exterior. The metal crunched and squealed with the impacts, echoing around the empty forest along with the sound of the racing engines.

"Brent," Carly said breathlessly. "We need to get back onto the road."

"I know, I know. I'm looking for a way out. Call the police. Tell them we're being pursued in the forest adjacent to the Mountain Retreat Diner."

He watched her pull out her cell phone with shaky hands and place the call. In the meantime, the headlights of his truck were picking out the trees up ahead and he had to react quickly, twisting and turning with sharp movements, all the while scanning for a forest lane or footpath that would lead them back to the road. The lights of the SUV behind him were dazzling, and every now and then, the vehicle would get close enough to touch his bumper, sending him skipping forward. But he was managing to snake around the trees successfully, using his headlights and the light dappling through the leaves to navigate through the darkness.

Then his good fortune ran out. The hood of the car collided with a slender trunk that he just hadn't seen, due to its silvery color. The airbags exploded in the interior and they both jolted forward in their seats. He heard the seat belts lock in place, holding them fast, and a low hiss began to sound from somewhere under the hood.

"Take your gun and let's go." He punched Carly's seat belt to unfasten. "Don't think. Don't hesitate. Don't ask questions. Just run."

He jumped from the vehicle, pulling his weapon from its holster. The SUV had stopped just behind them and he saw a man slide from the driver's seat wearing a ski mask. Odell appeared from the passenger side just a second later, having obviously decided to dispense with any kind of mask this time around. Brent was momentarily stunned to see that Odell was holding a powerful assault rifle, which was capable of inflicting horrific damage. To gain the upper hand, Brent quickly took aim and fired, sending both men diving for cover behind their open car doors. His gun was no match for an assault rifle, and their only hope lay with outrunning their attackers and finding shelter.

"Come on." He yanked on the sleeve of Carly's blouse as she appeared next to him, her phone still in her hand. "We have to go."

They both set off running, kicking up the leaves and twigs of the forest floor. He heard the *pop-pop-pop* of the assault rifle behind them and the bullets slamming into the thick trunks that surrounded them. Brent had deliberately selected the largest trees to run through, creating an effective barrier between them and the shooter. He took a risk at glancing behind. The masked man was close, but Odell was much farther back, his rifle resting on the hood of the SUV for stability.

Another series of bullets rang out. The man in the mask cried out in anguish and fell heavily to the ground. Odell had shot his accomplice by mistake, and he yelled out a series of expletives in frustration. Then he snatched up his rifle and began his pursuit. Having chased Odell through his neighbors' backyards, Brent knew this guy ran like a greyhound. They could not outrun him, not in a million years.

"There!" He pointed to a barn in a clearing. "Let's get inside."

Carly was already ahead of him, thankfully wearing flat shoes and practical pants that day. She reached the barn, pushed open the doors and waited for him to catch up. Once they were both safely inside, Brent heaved the large doors closed, lifted the plank of wood that secured them in place and looked around for anything that would help them repel the danger.

Carly waited for her eyes to adjust to the darkness in the unused barn. When she was finally able to take in the scene, it was like something from a horror movie, with old and rusted farming tools hanging from the rafters. There was an ancient tractor in the corner with deflated tires and a missing hood. Tubes from the stripped engine were spilling out like entrails, and she wondered if this terrible place was where her life would end.

"No, please, Lord," she said. "Not like this."

"Where's the gun I gave you?" Brent asked, while dragging some wooden pallets to stack against the doors.

"I didn't bring it with me today." In her mind, she saw it sitting in the gun cabinet, where she had placed it after her firearms lesson with Brent. "I left it in the gun safe in the living room."

A look of irritation passed across his face.

"I asked you to put it in the glovebox," he said. "I thought it was there this whole time."

Brent had remained with his vehicle while Carly had gone into the courthouse. He'd mentioned the need to safeguard her weapon, so she knew he'd assumed she'd brought it. And she'd said nothing at the time in order to avoid an argument.

Yet she now realized her error. "I'm sorry."

Brent continued to stack whatever materials he could find against the entrance of the barn—boxes, empty oil drums, a corroded animal trough. Although Carly had agreed to keep Tamsin's old gun in her possession, she still didn't like holding it. The thought of actually firing a shot filled her with dread. She had only relented to Brent's request because it had seemed important to him that she was armed. He didn't understand why guns scared her.

"The cops are on their way, right?" Brent asked, pulling his cell from his pocket. "If they get here soon, we won't need the extra weapon anyway."

While she nodded an affirmative, he called 911 to update the dispatcher on their location, giving details of where they came off the road and where to find his vehicle. Just as he was reiterating that they were holed up in an abandoned barn close to his damaged pickup, a series of bullets peppered the door, creating a spray of wood splinters as the pallets and boxes broke apart. Brent grabbed Carly's arm and ushered her to the old tractor, using its bulk as a shield. Then he returned fire, leading to a sudden silence as Odell ceased shooting.

"Clarence!" Brent yelled out. "Don't do this. If you have any love left for Noah and Ruby, you'll stop hurting them."

His request was answered with another spray of bullets, this time all around them, as Odell skirted around the barn, possibly trying to find a weak spot for easy entry. Carly covered her ears with her hands, crouching to the hard and dusty ground to pray.

"Lord, I know I haven't talked to You much lately," she said with her eyes squeezed tightly shut. "And I'm sorry about that. I thought You'd abandoned me because of what happened to Laurie." She hastily brushed away a tear. "But the truth is that I abandoned You."

She felt Brent's warm hand touch the nape of her neck and let it rest there. In the distance, the distinctive wail of a siren could now be heard. Odell must've heard it too because, with one final burst of bullets on the exterior wall, his quick footsteps indicated he was fleeing the scene. Carly sagged with relief, as Brent put his arms around her and pulled her to her feet.

"It's okay," he said. "It looks like the Lord heard your prayer."

"I didn't even ask to be rescued. I just got a sudden urge to tell God that I was sorry for being angry."

"That's all He ever wants to hear," Brent said, brushing her hair aside with an index finger. "Because when we stop being angry, that's when He's able to help us the most."

Carly had never been so thankful to be home. Except she wasn't home. Brent wasn't her husband and Noah and Ruby weren't her children. Yet, being back at the cabin felt like a family environment to her. The children had both rushed into Brent's arms upon their arrival and he'd scooped them up in unison to hold them tight, while she looked on with a mixture of both joy and sadness. She would never get to feel these strong emotional attachments, because children weren't part of her future. Even if she changed her mind about having kids, at the age of thirty-eight she'd probably left it too late to find somebody and settle down. She'd just have to accept her life choices.

On seeing her hanging on the edges of their family reunion, Brent reached for her hand and pulled her into the hug. With the children now between them like the filling in a sandwich, Brent let out a sigh of satisfaction.

"This is nice, huh?" he said. "We missed you guys, right, Carly?"

She smiled. Brent was considerate to include her. "We sure did," she said. "It was a long and boring day and we talked about you all the time."

They broke apart and allowed Noah and Ruby to slowly slide to their feet. Keeping the ever-present danger out of the children's lives was still important, so she and Brent had agreed to say nothing about their biological father launching an attack. After the local police had arrived at the barn, they'd searched for Odell but he'd made a swift getaway in the SUV, having taken the opportunity to escape while the cops had still been a fair distance away. He'd left behind the body of a dead accomplice once again. At the police station, she and Brent had given detailed statements about what had happened and were then provided with a replacement car by the Cheyenne Police Department to continue their journey to Pinedale. It was an inconspicuous silver sedan that Brent insisted be checked over for location trackers before taking it. They couldn't take any chances.

Brent eyed the clock. "It's super late, so it's time for you kids to get to bed. Go brush your teeth with Uncle Amir and I'll come read you a story and tuck you in."

They headed to the doorway, where Amir was waiting to take their hands. As they disappeared from view, Liam entered the kitchen, holding a piece of paper on which Carly could see a phone number and the words *US Marshals Service*, followed by her name.

"The Wyoming Department of Family Services is concerned for your safety," he told her. "When they were informed about what happened after your court appearance in Cheyenne today, the head of the organization contacted the US Marshals Service to request official protection. The Marshals are already providing protection for Zoe Buchannan and her baby in a secret location, and they've agreed to include you in this arrangement." He handed the paper to Carly. "If you call this number, a marshal will come collect you within a few hours."

Carly looked down at the paper. Her boss must be assuming that she was being targeted by Kendall Buchannan because of her involvement in the custody battle between him and his wife. That's why they were offering her a place in Zoe Buchannan's safe house.

"What do you think, Carly?" Brent's face appeared to be crestfallen as if he was disappointed at the possibility of her leaving. "Would you rather be under the care of the Marshals instead of taking your chances with me?"

She didn't even need to take a second to consider it. "No. You've never failed me since I've been with you. I feel completely safe in your hands."

He nodded with a small smile. "That's good to hear." He rubbed at his trimmed beard. "Although I'm confused about something."

"What?"

He sat at the kitchen table, asking Liam to give them some time alone. Carly felt a sense of dread descending. Why did he need privacy? What was he about to say? She remained standing while he spoke.

"It's great that you have confidence in my ability to take care of you while you're facing danger from Odell, but at the same time you have reservations about my ability to create a safe home environment for Noah and Ruby." He looked up at her. "It makes no sense. I'm either a strong protector or I'm not. So which one is it?"

Her stomach lurched. He had just exposed a deep flaw in her reasoning for taking her time in approving the adoption. He *was* capable of taking care of his children and shielding them from harm. She knew in her heart that he would not commit the same heinous act that Oliver Dowd had carried out against his newly adopted daughter. Yet, she couldn't persuade her head to accept what her heart already knew. It was an internal battle that she couldn't control.

"I never said that I had reservations about your ability to create a safe environment for the children," she said.

He laughed softly. "Oh, come on, Carly. You

might not have said it with actual words, but you imply it all the time. Your firearms questionnaire is a good example. You have doubts about me. I just want you to admit it."

The person she doubted the most was herself. If only she could bring herself to say it, Brent might understand her better. He might even be kind and compassionate and help her to heal. Or he might be horrified that she had placed a child with a man who went on to murder her. It was all too personal and painful to go into detail. She hadn't even sorted out her feelings for herself, so she couldn't begin to articulate them to somebody else.

"You've got me all wrong, Brent. I actually like you a lot. I've never met a man like you before. You're respectful and sweet, but you're no pushover. You take the time to truly listen, especially with Noah and Ruby. Those kids have been through so much in their short lives and you've given them a wonderful home that's full of love. I enjoy being with you because you fill every room with warmth, and you make me feel like the world is a safe place again."

"Again?" He stood up. "Did something happen to make you think that the world wasn't safe?"

She crossed her arms, realizing she had

gone further than she intended. "I don't want to talk about it."

He walked to her and stood close. "Who is Laurie?"

She flinched at the mention of the name, giving no reply.

"You mentioned her when you were praying in the barn," he continued. "You told God that you thought He'd abandoned you because of what happened to Laurie. Is she the reason why you don't think the world is a safe place? Is she the reason why you can't let go of your fears about Noah and Ruby being hurt?"

"Please, Brent. Please don't ask me about Laurie." Tears welled in her eyes. "I can't talk about it."

"Why?"

The tears began to fall. "Because it hurts."

He gathered her into his arms, rubbing her back and shoulders, letting her weep into his chest.

"When we go through trauma, it can take a while to heal," he said. "But you'll never heal unless you face it head-on. Otherwise, it'll just circle round and round in your head and never be resolved."

She stared at him, blinking fast. He had just described her life since the tragedy. Laurie was often the last person on Carly's mind as she drifted off to sleep at night. She had relived every meeting, every conversation and every little detail relating to Laurie's adoption case. Brent was right. She was stuck in a loop that would never be resolved.

He wound his fingers through her hair at the base of her neck and held her head with a gentle hand.

"I don't know what you're so afraid to tell me, but it can't be worse than carrying it inside. You said that you feel safe with me, so why not take a chance on trusting me with your worst fears?"

Brent sounded just like her coworkers, who had implored her to get some help when it became clear that she had been left traumatized. Her boss had offered to book counseling sessions in the aftermath of the murder, but she had refused. For a long time, the mere thought of discussing Laurie made her feel physically sick. She had assumed that the pain and fear would dissipate over time, but if anything, it had gotten worse. The shame and guilt only grew stronger.

It was that sense of guilt that now guided her words. "I made a terrible mistake a while ago, but I'd rather you didn't know about it. I'd actually rather not discuss it with anybody. It makes me feel ashamed. I have to live with the blame for what happened because I deserve to suffer."

"You're wrong." He held her tighter. "You don't deserve to suffer. I wish you'd trust me enough to tell me why you feel this way." She felt his heart rate quicken beneath his denim shirt. "There's a connection between us. I know you feel it too."

He was right. She *did* feel a special connection to him, and it was particularly strong at that moment. However, it wasn't strong enough to override the small voice in her head that warned her off. She placed two flat palms on his chest and firmly pushed, forcing him to take a step backward.

"I'm your adoption caseworker," she said, wiping the wetness that remained beneath her eyes. "I shouldn't be getting close to you like this. I should be maintaining a professional distance." She took a deep breath. "I'm sorry. Please forget the name Laurie and forget everything I just told you."

"How can I do that when it's obvious you're hurting?"

"I'll be fine. I'll try to pick up speed on your adoption case. That's what you really want, isn't it?"

"Yes," he said. "But I also want you to be happy."

She raised her eyes to the ceiling, trying to remember the last time she was really, truly happy. Then it struck her—the morning she had spent with Noah, Ruby and Brent making the ocean collage had allowed her to experience unbridled joy for the first time in five months. Brent had opened up a door that had been closed for such a long time, and she adored being in the midst of his family. But it was all based on a pretense. He didn't know what she had done, and if he found out, the special connection he'd spoken about would be severed. It was best to keep quiet.

Brent was a wonderful man. He was reminding her of this fact every day. All she needed to do was grit her teeth, push down her fears and get the adoption paperwork submitted to the court. Then she could return to her lonely single life and forget about him.

Noah and Ruby slept late the following morning, a rare occurrence for which Brent was thankful, as it gave him time to sit quietly with his Bible to pray. He needed this time to get his head straight. He felt as though he'd made a breakthrough with Carly the previous evening, only for the shutters to be yanked down once again. He now didn't know how to proceed. Should he continue to gently question her in the hope that she would confide in him? Or would this backfire? Perhaps the overriding focus in his life should remain solely on adopting Noah and Ruby. He didn't want anything to jeopardize this process, not even a woman who often took his breath away.

With so much weighing on his mind, Brent had been grateful to unburden himself and submit to the Lord's authority. He rolled his shoulders, feeling lighter and freer. Throughout his life, in both good and bad times, his faith had been steadfast. The quiet morning had provided a perfect opportunity to read Scripture and be reminded to trust in God's power. He had also taken a few moments to pray for Carly's faith to be strengthened, as he thought that she would benefit from intercession.

His cell began to buzz on the dining room table, where it lay next to his open Bible. The number on the display belonged to the Pinedale Fire Department, and he answered the call with the hope of hearing good news.

"Hey, Norm. What have you got for me?"

Following Brent's lead, the chief dispensed with formalities and got straight to the point.

"I've received a report from the Arson Investigation Team relating to the fire at the apartment block. They didn't manage to locate any security footage or fingerprints. Our suspect most likely scouted out the place beforehand and used an entrance that wasn't under surveillance."

As Brent's hopes of good news faded away, the chief followed up with something that lifted them back up immediately.

"But what the team *did* manage to find was DNA that almost certainly belongs to the perp."

"DNA? That's great. How did you get it?"

"One of the investigators discovered a discarded gas container in a dumpster close to the building. The arsonist must've nicked his skin through his gloves at some point because there were tiny traces of blood and wool fibers on the container's handle. We got the sample fast-tracked through the lab and it revealed a full DNA profile."

"Did the Arson Unit run it through the police database?"

"They did and no match was found."

Brent wasn't overly surprised. "If that's Odell's DNA on the handle then we won't get a match on our database because he's never been required to provide a sample. He's been as slippery as a snake over the years, always managing to stay out of prison by using smart-aleck lawyers who paint him as a family man who desperately wants to give up his criminal lifestyle and turn his life around. My guess is that the DNA on that gas container belongs to Odell, and once we have a sample from him, we can add the crime of arson to his arrest warrant."

"I hope he gets picked up soon, Sheriff. And wherever you are, I pray you stay safe. I know it must be difficult for you to be away from the town, but you're doing a great job in looking after your kids. Are you any closer to getting the adoption finalized?"

Brent gritted his teeth. He had no idea how close he was to being Noah and Ruby's legal father. It could take another two weeks, two months or two years. He was entirely reliant on Carly Engelman, and she was a law unto herself.

"I'm not sure about timetables," he replied honestly. "But I've put my trust in the process, and everything will work out as it's meant to."

"You're obviously meant to be a daddy," the chief said, as Carly came into the dining room, carrying a tray with coffee and pancakes. "Everybody in Pinedale can see that."

"That's kind of you, Norm. Thanks for the call. I appreciate it."

He hung up and quickly gave Carly a run-down of the new development. It looked like Odell's arrest warrant might soon contain an arson charge alongside attempted kidnapping, attempted murder, manslaughter, reckless endangerment, assault and a whole host of traffic offenses. All they needed was a DNA sample from him to match to the arsonist. Once Odell was in custody, there would be no wriggling out of prison time on these charges. He was facing the rest of his life behind bars. That was why his determination to snatch Noah and Ruby made no sense to Brent. Even if Odell managed to succeed, he would never be able to live normally again. He would have to spend every day looking over his shoulder, forced to go on the run whenever the authorities got too close.

Unless he had plans to smuggle the children out of the country somehow. Only Odell himself knew of the rationale behind his actions. Brent could merely guess.

"I've been working on your adoption file this morning," Carly said, pouring two cups of coffee from the pot. "I woke at five a.m. so I decided to put the time to good use."

He was pleasantly surprised. "What is there left to do?"

"Not much. We've done all the hard stuff

already. I now need to prepare a case file for the judge and book a court slot for him or her to review it. Once they see that everything has been handled in accordance with state law, they'll award permanent legal custody to you. It's called a finalization hearing, and once it's over, the children are yours forever."

Brent's stomach exploded in a swirl of excitement. This was the first time Carly had spoken so openly about the end of this process. The thought of standing in a courtroom to hear a judge award him permanent fatherly status was enough to bring emotion rushing to the surface. This would be the culmination of a long and difficult time, during which the children had endured the loss of their foster mother and an adjustment to a new life. They would finally be a legally recognized family.

"So I meet the standard?" he asked tentatively. "I wasn't sure which way you would fall."

"I know I've taken my time with this," she said, adding sugar to her coffee and stirring, keeping her focus on the cup. "But I'm trying really hard to do the right thing by you and the children."

"You didn't answer my question." He dragged his chair closer to hers. "Did I pass the test?"

She placed her spoon on the tray and swiveled to face him. "As a father, yes."

Brent's earlier resolve to focus solely on the adoption process now began to dissolve. Carly was wearing a faded denim shirt with the collar open to reveal a small silver cross resting in the dip of her throat. With her hair piled up hastily in a claw clip, she was messy and beautiful, and he couldn't help himself.

"Do you also see me as someone you could learn to trust? Could you take a chance on me being more than a friend?"

She took a long time to respond, but stared deep into his eyes in the silence.

"I'm not sure," she said finally. "But my heart is telling me to kiss you right now."

He placed his hand on her cheek. "Well, we have to give the heart what it wants, right?"

She smiled. "I guess so."

When their lips met, Brent found that it felt so natural and right. Their mouths seemed to be totally in tune with each other's, moving rhythmically and effortlessly. He felt her fingers snake through his belt loops, as she seemed to relax into him. Could she be letting go of her fears at last? Was this the start of something special?

SEVEN

Carly had never felt this way before, as if she truly belonged in Brent's arms. The way he was kissing her was soft, gentle and wonderful, and each and every muscle in her body relaxed with the feeling of being loved.

Then a sudden thought occurred to her: she didn't want to be loved. She had devoted her whole existence to taking care of defenseless children. Falling for a man wasn't part of her plan. As if a switch had been flipped, this intimate moment with Brent now felt all wrong, and she pulled away quickly, pushing back her chair to put some space between them.

"What's the matter?" he asked. "Did I do something wrong?"

She stood up. "No. I just realized that we shouldn't be doing this."

"Why not?"

"Because we hardly know each other."

He balked. "That's not true. You've raked

through my entire life with a fine-tooth comb. You've asked me every kind of question under the sun and probed into every dark corner of my home. I've hidden nothing from you, Carly, so I think you must know me better than any person in the whole world."

She took a step backward, unable to refute his assertion. She probably did know him better than anybody else. But *he* didn't know *her*. He didn't know her terrible secret, and this fact put a yawning chasm between them. She had been foolish to think there could be something special between them. She didn't deserve happiness. There was a little girl who would never grow into a woman because of her, and she could only atone for this injustice by remaining steadfast and resolute in her commitment to her job. It was hard to move past her tragic error, but she would never make things right by selfishly pursuing Brent.

"You are a client of the Department of Family Services," she said, backing away from him. "And I'm your caseworker. There should be a professional boundary between us at all times. I could be fired for this."

It was true that relationships between clients and caseworkers were forbidden, but Carly was guilty of exaggerating the repercussions. If she reported this lapse to her boss, he would likely tell her to await the adoption completion before exploring the possibility of a relationship, but he definitely wouldn't invoke a punishment. He would probably be happy for her.

"I'm sorry," Brent said. "I didn't realize the implications of us getting close. It's just that I can't help myself. I have these feelings for you that keep getting stronger." He looked down at his feet. "But I guess you're right. The adoption should be the priority in both our lives. This won't happen again."

"It's for the best. You don't know what you'd be getting yourself into."

Brent laid out the pieces of a jigsaw puzzle on the coffee table in the living room and sat, cross-legged, on the floor with Noah and Ruby. The court judge who had loaned him the cabin had a number of grandchildren, so there were board games, puzzles and books dotted around the place. These were thankfully keeping Noah and Ruby occupied. Brent had started allowing them to play in the backyard for short intervals under close supervision. This used up some of their physical energy, but they required mental stimulation too. Hence, most of Brent's time on that day had been taken up with indoor activities.

Carly had retreated to her office to work on the adoption report, but he guessed she was avoiding him. The kiss they'd shared early in the morning must have affected her in the same intense way it had affected him. There was no way she hadn't felt a similarly powerful attraction. Kisses like that didn't just happen out of nowhere. They were one in a million.

"Daddy Brent," Ruby said, tugging on his shirtsleeve. "Did you catch our other daddy yet? The bad daddy in the clown mask."

Brent busied himself with looking at the pieces of the puzzle, ensuring that his tone remained calm and comforting. This was the first time either of the children had mentioned their birth father since the day he'd tried to snatch them. To make them feel safe, he needed to play down the threat.

"We didn't catch him yet, Ruby," he said. "But we're close. He won't hurt you."

Noah stopped rifling through the puzzle pieces to stare at Brent with his big blue eyes. "Do you promise?"

"I promise." He leaned across the table and planted a kiss on the boy's head. "I'm your daddy now, and I will always take care of you."

Ruby tilted her head to the side, the way

she always did when asking a question that perplexed her.

"Why do we have two daddies?"

Noah jumped in with an answer before Brent could think of a response.

"Because the first daddy messed up after our first mommy died. He didn't give us dinner or take us to school, so the police didn't let him be a daddy anymore. Then Brent and Tamsin got the job as our new mommy and daddy." He dropped his head. "Except Tamsin died too, so now Brent looks after us by himself."

Brent's heart lurched to hear Noah talking about this. Noah remembered a lot more about their previous life than his sister. He had spoken about his experiences often after first joining Brent's household, but it had gradually lessened as he'd become more confident and secure. He and his sister had taken the death of Tamsin in stride, sadly not having had the opportunity to form a long-term bond with her. He wished they had a mother figure in their lives. No matter how great a father he was, he could never replace a mother's love.

"I'm not going anywhere," Brent said, wanting to give them a shot of reassurance.

"Even if a big monster tried to chase me away, I would never ever leave you."

Ruby giggled and raised a little fist in the air. "I can bash a big monster if he chases you. I'm superstrong."

"Of course you are," Brent said with a wink. "You beat me at arm wrestling all the time."

Noah rolled his eyes. "You let her win."

Ruby jumped up and stamped her foot. "He does *not* let me win."

As the children began bickering, Brent picked them up, one under each arm, and tickled them in unison until they screamed with laughter. Then he placed them back on their feet and sat on the floor between them.

"I want you both to know that I'm really happy to be your daddy," he said. "You used to have a different daddy, but he couldn't look after you like I can, so he's not in your life anymore. He did some bad things, which makes me sad, but you don't need to be worried or scared, because you have me, Uncle Amir and Uncle Liam here with you."

"And Carly," Ruby added. "I like her. She's nice. And she's pretty."

"I like her too, and not just because she's pretty, but because she's kind and she helped me become your new daddy."

All this talk of fathers must have given Ruby a lot to think about. "What *is* a daddy?"

Oh boy! These questions were really difficult this morning. As he struggled to find the right words to formulate in response, he noticed Carly standing in the doorway, watching them with interest. He had no idea how long she'd been there, but she was smiling.

She came into the room giving an answer to Ruby's question on his behalf. "A daddy is somebody who loves you with arms that reach up to the sky." She stretched her hands to the ceiling, and Ruby giggled while Noah copied the movement. "If you fall over, a daddy will pick you up and hold you tight. If you do something wrong or make a mistake, a daddy will teach you how to do it better next time. A daddy will show you how to ride a bike and build a fort. He'll throw you in the air and always catch you on the way down. He helps with homework and book reading and sports."

"And splinters?" Ruby interrupted, holding up an index finger.

Carly and Brent laughed together. "Oh, for sure," she said. "A daddy is always the best at dealing with splinters."

Brent scooted over to his daughter and took her by the hand to inspect her finger. Sure enough, there was a tiny piece of wood embedded just beneath the skin. She winced as he touched it.

"I was crawling in the hallway, meowing and being a kitty-cat," she said. "And the floor bit me."

"If you hold still, I can make it better." Brent used his fingernails to pinch the splinter's end, and with one flicking movement it was dislodged and discarded. "There you go. All done. If you want to be a cat again, find some gloves, okay?"

Brent leaned behind his daughter and grabbed some antiseptic wipes from the dresser. Ruby sucked air through her teeth as he wrapped a moist wipe around the sore finger and held it tight. Meanwhile, Carly sat next to Noah on the couch and began piecing together the jigsaw puzzle. Noah looked up at her, smiling, and in that one brief moment Brent saw a deep attachment between them. Carly had been a constant in the children's lives since removing them from Odell's home. She had rescued them, comforted them and found them a new home. It was little wonder that Noah gazed at her with such strong affection. She was a hero to him. She was a hero to hundreds of kids.

Losing Carly from their lives wouldn't only be difficult for Brent but it would be a wrench for the children too. They'd all grown to love her without realizing. He found himself fantasizing about how wonderful their lives would be in a family of four, with Carly there every evening to share dinner and laugh at the kids' antics. She would complete his life.

No, he told himself silently. *You know that's not gonna happen.*

With the adoption so close to completion, he shouldn't rock the boat and potentially make waves. Besides, Carly had made her position clear. She wasn't interested in him as anything more than a client.

Something else was also troubling him. Since sharing a kiss with Carly, a sense of disloyalty had been niggling in his head. Brent had loved Tamsin so very much, and to find himself attracted to another woman so soon after her death was surely wrong. He was mindful of hurting Tamsin's family or sullying her memory by appearing to move on without a second thought. This was a complex situation in many ways. The last thing he wanted to do was make it worse.

He would let sleeping dogs lie.

Loneliness was an emotion that Carly had always managed to keep at bay with a heavy work schedule. Whenever she found herself feeling sad and alone, she would pick up a case file and immerse herself in an adoption or fostering assignment, or pore over notes taken during a child protection meeting. There was always something to distract her and take her mind off the fact that nobody was at her side when she sat down to eat dinner or watch a movie.

But then Laurie was killed and she found herself unable to rely on those distraction tactics any longer. Since opting for part-time hours, she had more time on her hands to ponder her future. She questioned herself constantly, wondering whether she still had the appropriate level of skill required to be a child protection officer. Lately, she found every little decision torturous, whereas she was previously supremely confident in her ability to make the right call. Her job was beginning to weigh her down, as each day seemed to get harder and harder. Returning to full-time hours wasn't an option, as she simply couldn't bring herself to face taking on a greater workload. She definitely couldn't go back to overseeing adoption cases. Once Brent's file was passed to the court for authorization, she would never put herself in that position again. The scars on her heart were too wide, and the guilt too deep.

A soft knock sounded on the open door and she glanced up to see Brent staring at her, his expression tender and gentle. The way he looked at her often pushed her off balance emotionally, as if he wanted to hold her close.

"I'm here to say thank you for that amazing speech you gave to the kids about what it means to be a father," he said. "It was beautiful. It actually brought a tear to my eye."

She smiled. "When you've dealt with as many fathers as I have, you learn to recognize what traits are the best ones."

He came into the room and pointed to a plastic folder on the desk. "Is that my adoption file?"

She tapped the label on the front, where the name FOX was written above the case number that had been allocated by the Department of Family Services.

"I just requested a finalization hearing date from the Sublette County District Court," she said. "I'm hoping to hear back from them within a few days. The paperwork has been submitted online and you'll have my full support on the day of the hearing."

A huge smile broke across Brent's face and he made an approach with his arms wide, as if he was going to hug her. At the last second, he stopped and let his arms drop, reading her body language. She didn't feel in a celebratory mood, despite the positive step.

"I don't know what's been going on in your life," he said. "But you've obviously been dealing with a personal situation while overseeing my adoption case. I'm not gonna lie, your attitude has made me angry with you at times and I've probably been guilty of being insensitive. You've overcome a lot of insecurity to get this far and I'm grateful. I'm sorry if I've been pigheaded."

"These are your children, Brent," she said. "You're allowed to be pigheaded when it comes to fighting in their corner."

"I know it sounds stupid, but I was worried that you thought I'd do something awful to the kids once the process was complete. I mean *really* awful. Like murder them in their beds or something."

She stared at him, a lump forming in her throat. She repeatedly tried to swallow it away but it refused to budge, and moisture quickly rushed to her eyes. Brent was clearly expecting her to wave away his ludicrous suggestion with a laugh, or at least appear shocked. Instead, she bowed her head, trying to surreptitiously wipe away her tears.

"I'll let you know when the hearing date

is scheduled." She couldn't prevent her voice from breaking. "I think we're done for now."

He didn't move, and she waited in agonizing silence as he watched her begin to weep behind her desk. Then, without a word, he walked to the windowsill and plucked a tissue from a box sitting there, before handing it to her and kneeling next to her chair. She took the tissue and used it to cover her eyes. For Brent to see this moment of weakness was mortifying. She wished he would leave. But he stayed.

"I don't think we're done," he said quietly. "In fact, I think we only just got started."

"I'm sorry," she said between jerky breaths. "I'll be fine. Go be with your kids."

"They're playing dress-up with Liam," he said. "And I'd rather be here with you than have toilet paper wound around my arms and legs."

Brent always managed to make her laugh, even when she was at her lowest ebb. "Are the kids turning him into a mummy?"

"They sure are. And they're loving every minute of it."

He waited while she steadied her breathing and composed herself. Then he asked her the one question she dreaded most in the world.

"What happened in your last adoption case?"

Her mind raced as she tried to come up with an answer that would avoid telling lies but would also sidestep the query. Eventually, she gave up. She was exhausted with the pretense.

"I messed up," she said, wringing the tissue in her fingers. "I made a mistake that can never be undone. A child is dead because of me."

"Was her name Laurie?"

"Yes. Her name was Laurie Stephens and she was the sweetest kid you could ever meet." Laurie's face settled on Carly's mind. "She had a million freckles and a huge smile. She was always laughing, which was a testament to her character because that kid had the hardest start in life. Her mom frequently left her alone to look after her younger siblings for days at a time, even though she was only eight years old. But she did her best, and she fed her sisters, bathed them and played games. We only found out about her situation after she got caught stealing food from a convenience store. The police went to her home to speak to her mom and discovered that the three kids were by themselves. None of them could read or write because they'd never been enrolled at a school. I immediately got a court order to permanently remove them from the mother, and then I found them adoptive families."

"Did they stay together?"

"Sadly, no. It's often really hard to find homes for three siblings, so I had to split them up. I found a home for Laurie in Cheyenne, and her two sisters went to a nearby town called Orchard Valley. But the adoptive families agreed to meet up often and allow the sisters plenty of contact with each other. It seemed like an ideal solution."

"What went wrong?"

How could she tell him of her fatal error? It might change his entire perception of her. She was so ashamed and afraid.

He placed a hand on top of hers. "I'm guessing that you've never spoken about this before, so take your time."

She couldn't look him in the eye, but now that a brick had been removed from the wall, the whole structure came tumbling down, and the words fell from her mouth.

"I'd received an inquiry from a man in Cheyenne a few weeks before Laurie got taken into care. His name was Oliver Dowd. He and his wife, Nina, were both emergency care doctors at a city hospital. They were in their forties and wanted to adopt an older child. When I introduced them to Laurie, everything seemed to click into place. They adored each other right away. Nina planned to reduce her hours at work and be at home every day when Laurie got back from school. Oliver wanted to help her with her reading and make sure she reached her potential. I honestly thought Laurie would be safe with them. She deserved all the happiness in the world after everything she'd been through."

"I heard about this family on the news a few months back. Oh, Carly, I'm so sorry. Oliver Dowd killed his wife and daughter before turning the gun on himself."

The tears resurfaced. "That's right. It happened two weeks after the adoption got finalized. My knees buckled under me when I heard the news report. I was due to have a follow-up meeting with the Dowds later that day. I was planning on asking them if they would agree to be featured in one of our adoption brochures. I thought…" She stopped to let out a sob. "I thought I'd done a good job."

Brent squeezed her hand. "You *did* do a good job. You made a decision based on the information that was available at the time. You could never have foreseen what would happen."

"Couldn't I?"

She withdrew her hand from his and stood up, walking to the window. It was a breezy day and the tall trees in the forest swayed, rippling in waves of lush green foliage. She concentrated on watching the scenery for a while, not sure whether she wanted Brent to embrace her or leave her alone. She craved his comfort but didn't believe she was worthy.

"Mr. Dowd had no history of violence or threatening behavior," she said. "But there must have been other subtle signs that I missed. He sometimes worked long shifts and was tired. That might've affected his judgment. He was a little absentminded and his paperwork was untidy. He even snapped at his wife once. I didn't notice those red flags."

She felt Brent's hands pressing on her shoulders, just firm enough to calm her.

"What you're describing is a perfectly normal man," he said. "Working long shifts, being untidy and snapping at your wife on occasion aren't red flags. If they were, millions of men would be on watch lists. The truth is much harder for you to swallow because it means you couldn't have prevented this from happening. Oliver Dowd killed his family for reasons that we will never know. I remember the Cheyenne police chief saying that nobody saw it coming, not his parents, his colleagues or even his therapist."

She tensed up. "You shouldn't be giving me a free pass on this, Brent. You should be harder on me."

He sighed. "I couldn't possibly be any harder on you than you are on yourself."

"Let's say you're right. Let's say that I couldn't have prevented this tragedy from happening." She turned around and gazed up at him. "If that's true, you know what it means, right?"

"I do." He held her face with his two hands. "It means you can't stop it from happening again."

She let out a cry, having been forced to face her worst fear. Her superpower was saving children from harm, and now she felt stripped of that power. Letting her forehead rest on Brent's chest, she closed her eyes and cried. A smell of woodsmoke rose from his shirt, embedded into the fabric after he laid the fire that morning. She gripped the shirt hems and held them fast, while Brent slid his arms round her neck to embrace her tenderly.

"You do a great job in a world that isn't always fair," he whispered into her ear. "Don't let Oliver Dowd define you."

"It's too late," she mumbled into his torso. "He already did."

Brent couldn't sleep. All he could think about was Carly. Everything she had said and done to put obstacles in his path during this adoption process now made sense. She had been left scarred by the murder-suicide carried out by Oliver Dowd. The incident had sent shock waves through the police department in Cheyenne at the time, and Brent remembered the revulsion felt by law enforcement officers across the state.

The killing of a child was always a difficult fact to accept, but especially when a young life was ended by the hand of a parent. Parents were tasked with protecting their children, so Oliver Dowd's actions flew in the face of the natural order of things.

Mr. Dowd's life had been raked over by the news outlets in the aftermath in order to uncover his reasons, but nothing conclusive came to light. He had given no indication of his intentions and had shot his wife and daughter at point-blank range while they slept in their beds one night. The coroner ruled that they likely wouldn't have suffered or even awoken beforehand. That was a small blessing in the tragedy.

What Brent hadn't realized until now was that Carly had been involved in the Dowds' adoption case. And she had carried the burden of guilt on her shoulders ever since. He was glad she had finally taken a risk on trusting him, but this didn't mean his adoption case was a sure thing. While she had agreed to support him for the time being, she could easily change her mind. Until the judge awarded him permanent custody, Carly could still create problems for him. Even though he longed to hold her in his arms and heal her wounded spirit, he was wary of upsetting the smooth path toward legal fatherhood. He was stuck between wanting to be a permanent daddy to his kids and helping a woman he was growing to care deeply about. There was no easy solution.

He heard the creak of a floorboard rising from somewhere in the cabin. Carly was most likely similarly struggling to sleep and was creeping downstairs for a mug of hot tea, which she often did late at night. Brent's shift on guard duty didn't begin until 4:00 a.m., and Amir was currently keeping watch on the porch at the front of the house. This cabin was really beginning to feel like a safe haven, hidden away from prying eyes and still unknown to Odell or anyone else who meant them harm. Sometimes, it even felt as though they were on a family vacation, with Carly being a mother figure in the children's daily lives. She played with them, read stories, cuddled them when they cried and gave them a talking-to when they deserved it. She had slid into the family so effortlessly that he often forgot she was just their adoption caseworker. She felt like so much more.

After turning over one last time, he finally admitted defeat and threw back the covers. Rising from bed in his pajamas, he pulled on a warm sweatshirt. The evenings were chilly in the forest and the cabin's temperature dropped significantly overnight. He decided to go check on the kids to see if they needed an extra blanket. He made a point to check on his kids every night. Ever since they had arrived in his home, he would peek into their rooms and marvel at how peacefully they slept, and he loved to see their sweet faces resting on the pillow.

Another creak sounded in the cabin, but this one was louder than the last. He reached for a key that he kept on a high ledge out of the children's grasp. Then he unlocked the gun cabinet in his room before taking out his gun and loading it. He told himself it was just a precaution. It was unlikely that an intruder could gain access, as he would've been noticed by Amir, but it didn't hurt to be prepared. He opened the door and peered out into the dark hallway. The lamp on the table by the window lit the hallway dimly, just enough to guide his footsteps. Stepping out onto the shined floorboard in his bare feet, he decided not to call out, just in case he woke the household.

But he needn't have been so cautious, because a sound echoed that would surely alert everyone. It was a scream. And it had come from Carly.

EIGHT

Carly stood in the doorway of Ruby's room, face to face with Odell. He was wide-eyed with surprise, having been caught red-handed carrying a sleeping Ruby in his arms. For a second or two Carly and Odell were both rooted to the spot, neither expecting to see the other. Carly had only popped her head through the door to check on Ruby, but had been taken off guard to see Odell lifting her from her bed and into his arms.

After coming to her senses, Carly opened her mouth and screamed.

Odell tried to push past her into the hallway, as Ruby stirred and began to wriggle and squirm. Carly held her ground and pushed back, noticing a gun in Odell's waistband that he was prevented from using because his arms were curled around Ruby.

"No," Carly said, trying to wrest the child from his grasp. "You won't take her."

Ruby woke fully, realized who had her and fought to be released. In a tangle of limbs, Carly grabbed hold of anything she came into contact with, pulling out a chunk of hair from Odell's scalp. He lashed out in pain, dropping Ruby onto her bed, after which she immediately jumped up and ran from the room, calling for Daddy Brent. In a flash, Brent was there, barreling into Odell as he made a movement to reach for his gun. They rolled over and over on the floor, with Brent landing blows onto Odell's face and chest. Carly ran into the hallway to find Ruby. The girl was at the top of the staircase but was scooped up quickly by Amir, who came bounding up the stairs in response to the commotion.

Handing Ruby to Carly, Amir said, "Go wake Noah and take both children to Liam. Where's Brent?"

She pointed. "Ruby's room. Odell broke in."

Brent's voice called from the other side of the door. "He's gone out the window. I'm going after him."

Liam then appeared in the hallway, having clearly just woken up but nevertheless alert and holding his gun.

"You go too, Amir," he said. "I'll stay with

Carly and the kids. Go find Odell and arrest him."

Amir vanished into Ruby's room and out the window. Carly heard Brent shout from somewhere outside, telling his deputy to follow him into the woods, where Odell was attempting to make his escape. Then silence descended. With Ruby curled around her torso, Carly stood in the hallway, realizing that one of her hands was balled tightly into a fist, her nails digging into her palm. She looked down and saw she was clutching a handful of sandy hair, ripped out by its roots. Odell had left a little piece of himself behind.

Brent ran through the woods in his bare feet, closely followed by Amir. They were tracking Odell through the trees, but there was precious little moonlight that night and the darkness enveloped them. The nocturnal sounds and movements of the forest could easily be mistaken for a person and he responded to each rustle and falling shadow by facing it as a threat. Bats, foxes and owls were highly active at night and their peace, as well as Brent's, had been disturbed by a man with evil intent.

"Over there," Amir said quietly, pointing

to a huge white ash tree. "Something's moving behind that trunk."

Holding his gun close to his body, Brent skirted around the side, directing Amir to go the other way, hoping to effect a pincer movement. Odell must have been watching the cabin for a while that evening, working out a way to get inside. He had used a ladder to climb up to Ruby's room and found a way to break the lock on the window. If Carly hadn't gone into the room when she did, the outcome could've been a lot different. This time, Odell seemed to be acting alone, but Brent still wanted to get back to the cabin as soon as possible, just in case this was a distraction tactic.

He stopped at the side of the tree and gave a nod to Amir. They moved in unison, jumping around the trunk, calling out an order to put hands in the air. But the space was empty, except for a badger that foraged in the leaves. Now startled and scared, the animal ran into the dark.

Brent holstered his weapon. His feet were burning from exposure to the cold ground.

"I think we should go back. This forest is huge and Odell could be anywhere. Besides, I don't like leaving Liam to guard the cabin alone."

"This is all my fault, boss," Amir said sorrowfully. "While I was on guard duty, I heard voices in the trees at the front of the house so I left my post to investigate. When I found a small radio balanced on a high branch, I knew I'd been duped. I'm so sorry."

Brent placed a reassuring hand on his subordinate's shoulder. "You did what you thought was best at the time, Deputy. Let's learn from it and remember to wake each other whenever there are signs of danger. We're a team, right?"

"Right."

Brent began walking through the woods, making for the cabin, with Amir close behind.

"I guess we'll need to move to a new location quickly," the deputy said. "Should we go right away?"

"I'll need to make some calls and arrange for a new safe house. We'll leave after the sun comes up." He clicked his tongue in frustration. "But first, I need to work out how we were found in the first place."

Brent closed the trunk of the car that had been loaned to him by the Cheyenne police after his pickup had been totaled. The vehicle was now full of their suitcases and ready to transport them to a new location. The only thing the car now didn't contain was a tracking device. After a very careful inspection that morning, Brent had found a small, battery-powered GPS tracker wedged deep down between the seats. How it had gotten there, he didn't know, but the Cheyenne Police Department had clearly failed to do its job. The police sergeant had promised him the loaned car had been inspected and was clean. Had Odell been watching the station and taken an opportunity to plant the tracker after the inspection, perhaps? Whatever the explanation, they were now exposed and vulnerable. With nothing to lose, Brent had stationed a couple of his deputies in cruisers close by. That would deter another attack if Odell got any ideas. But it made them conspicuous and he wanted to go off radar again.

"Hi." Carly came out of the cabin wearing jeans and a hooded sweatshirt. "Are we ready to go?"

"Almost. You and the children will travel with me, while Liam and Amir follow behind." He checked his watch. "Liam should be back in about thirty minutes. He went to Rock Springs early this morning to drop off Odell's hair sample at a forensics lab for DNA analysis. They agreed to fast-track it for us using rapid techniques. I'm obviously hoping that it will be a positive match for the DNA recovered at the scene of the arson attack. I want to make sure Odell has a ton of charges on his sheet to maximize his prison time."

"To get prison time, he has to be caught, and he sure is slippery."

"Tell me about it. He jumped from my grasp and out the window in a matter of seconds last night."

Brent leaned against the car, his body aching all over from his tussle with Odell. Although Brent had managed to land some strong blows, Odell had also thrown some punches in return. A dark bruise was now developing on Brent's bicep and a small cut was throbbing on his lip. Odell couldn't be underestimated. He might look like a lightweight, but he fought like a cat.

"I'm guessing that Odell's plan was to take Ruby first and then come back for Noah," she said. "He probably had an accomplice waiting close by."

"I should've realized how easy it would be to access Ruby's bedroom with a ladder and a screwdriver to pry open the window. I'm so thankful you went to check on her. I was about to do it myself, but I might've been a few seconds too late."

"It's a team effort here," she said. "We all have a part to play."

"How are the kids doing now?" he asked. "They seemed okay at breakfast, but they might be hiding their true feelings."

"They're fine." She waved away his concern. "I had a good, long talk with them this morning and they're actually taking this in stride. Ruby seems to think you're a cross between Superman and Captain America, so not only are you indestructible but you're capable of saving the life of every single person on the planet." She came to stand next to him and leaned on the car. "They both adore you, and they trust in your ability to protect them."

He slid his gaze sideways to meet hers. "What about you? What do you think?"

She smiled. "In my opinion, you're more of a Wolverine."

He splayed his fingers out wide. "Man, I need to trim my nails, huh?"

They laughed, and yet again, Brent found himself enjoying the time they were spending together. The guilt about moving on so quickly after Tamsin's death still remained, but it was lessening as he and Carly grew closer. Tamsin would want him to be happy.

"You know what I mean," he said. "Do you trust me to take care of you too?"

"Of course I do." She patted the waistband of her jeans, where a raised bump was visible beneath her red sweatshirt. "Although I'm not totally reliant on you because I've decided to carry the gun you gave me. I need to step up and be brave."

He slid a little way toward her and gently touched her pinkie with his own. He knew that carrying a weapon was a big deal for Carly. She had a very good reason to fear guns, especially with children around.

"You're quite a superhero yourself, you know that?" His admiration for her was growing along with his attraction. "I'd hire you as a deputy any day of the week."

"If you'd let me wear an actual superhero costume then I might just take you up on the offer."

"Are you thinking Wonder Woman?"

"I prefer Catwoman."

"Technically, Catwoman is a villain, so I'd have to fire you on your first day."

She made a face of mock indignation. "In that case, I'd come to your house and scratch up your furniture. And after that, I'd knock all the trinkets off your shelves one by one."

He laughed while holding up his hands in defeat. "No, please, anything but that."

She folded her arms and lifted her chin. "I

knew I'd break you eventually. Nobody ever wins a battle of wills against a cat."

Brent let his laughter fade away while watching Carly close her eyes to allow the sun to bathe her face. This was the first time he had seen her at peace with herself. He hoped she felt unburdened since telling him about Laurie. Perhaps she was finally shedding the blame she'd carried for far too long. Perhaps there was even a way forward for them.

"I still think about it, you know," he said.

She opened her eyes. "About what?"

"Our kiss."

She let her green eyes rest on him, scanning his face. "I think about it too."

"We just seem so good together, don't we? I mean, the attraction is clearly there, and we usually end up laughing like hyenas whenever we spend time together." He looked down at his feet, wondering whether he should be heading down this path. "I've developed some big feelings for you, Carly, and I don't know what to do with them."

"Focus on the adoption," she said without missing a beat. "You probably only feel this strongly because you're grateful to me for moving the process along."

"That's not true." He knew his own mind well enough to decipher his emotions. "I feel this way because you're an amazing and beautiful woman."

He saw her color rise, but she didn't respond to the compliment.

"When I became a child protection officer eighteen years ago, I promised myself I'd always give one hundred percent of my time and effort to my job. It's why I've never gotten married. I've never even been on a date. My life is my job, Brent."

"Have you ever considered changing your mind?"

She hesitated before saying, "No." She wasn't being truthful.

"Okay," he said. "I understand. I was also wary about taking our relationship to another level because I didn't want to rock the boat in the adoption process. But I'm starting to think that I might just be afraid."

"Of what?"

"Of making myself vulnerable. Of moving forward after losing Tamsin. Of loving someone again."

At the mention of the word *love*, Carly froze to the spot, her color rising even higher. This was obviously a turn in the conversation that gave her cause for concern.

"I have to go check my room to make sure

I didn't leave anything behind." She headed back inside. "Call me when it's time to leave."

"Sure." There was no point in pushing her beyond her comfort zone. "Thanks for the chat."

Carly sat on her bed, listening to the sound of birdsong through the open window. She was pretending to check her room before leaving, but she was hiding away like a coward. Her pulse was racing and her hands were trembling. Little by little, day by day, Brent was forcing her to question her decision to remain single. He was gently encouraging her to imagine what a life with him might be like. Their conversations were usually effortless and he was spot-on about the constant laughter. They seemed to be perfectly in tune with each other. They even liked the same movies, music and food. After a rocky start in their relationship, they were now like magnets being drawn together. A love was blossoming.

But would it all end in tears? Would Brent understand if she was required to rush from a date when a child needed an emergency care order? Would he allow her the freedom to spend entire evenings writing reports? Would he accept that he wasn't her number one priority?

That was doubtful. There was a reason why many of her colleagues were single or divorced. The stresses of the job took their toll, and a true dedication to children's advocacy involved personal sacrifice. Even with her part-time hours, she worked hard and was often on call. Her lifestyle was incompatible with Brent's. No amount of heart-stopping kisses would change that.

Her door creaked open an inch or two. Ruby was standing on the other side, clutching a stuffed rabbit. Wearing her favorite pink fleecy sweat suit, she looked about as cuddly as could be.

"Daddy Brent sent me to come get you," she said. "It's time to go."

Carly painted on a huge smile. "Okay, let's move on to the next adventure, huh?" She took Ruby by the hand. "Do you know where we're going?"

"I don't know for sure, but I think it might be big and cold." They walked down the stairs together. "I heard Daddy Brent say it was a castle."

At the bottom of the stairs, Brent smiled and put his hands on his hips, watching Carly and Ruby heading his way.

"I said it was next to a field of *cattle*, Ruby," he corrected. "Do you know what that is?"

"Umm." She screwed up her face. "Are they pretty flowers?"

"No." He bent down and pinched her cheek. "Cattle is what we call cows. Our new house is next to a field of cows."

"Yuck." She held her nose. "Smelly."

He poked the bulging tummy of her teddy bear. "Who's this guy? I don't remember him."

"He's a Charlie Bear who sits on the shelf in my room. His name is Bugsy and I want to take him with me."

Charlie Bear was Ruby's favorite brand of soft toys, and she had several of them at home, all different animals. Except she had decided to bring a doll to the cabin rather than one of her stuffed animals, which she'd regretted ever since.

Brent kneeled in front of her. "Bugsy probably belongs to the girl who uses that room when she sleeps over. We'll have to put him back."

Without warning, Ruby opened her mouth and began to wail, her voice rising and falling in a crescendo of noise. Carly was amazed that such a piercing sound could come from a girl of her small size.

"Let her take the bunny rabbit, Brent," she said, touching his arm. "We can bring it back when this is all over."

Brent picked up Ruby and held her in his arms. "Shh, it's okay. We'll take Bugsy with us and you can help him settle in his new room."

As Ruby's cries subsided, Brent patted and rubbed her back, while Carly headed into the kitchen to fill a glass of water. Her nerves were a little frazzled, not just because of the danger but because of her complicated situation with Brent.

"Are you okay?" he asked, coming into the kitchen, having handed a placated Ruby to Amir. "You look a little pale."

"It's probably dehydration. That's why I'm getting some water." She gulped down the cool liquid and set the cup in the sink. "Where are we headed?"

"It's a house just outside of Pinedale next to some farmland. Bryan arranged it for me."

"Bryan?"

"He's the pastor of my church. I called him early this morning to ask if we could stay in the church's halfway house. It's normally used for people who are recovering from alcohol or drug addiction, but it's currently empty. It's kind of off the beaten track, so it's ideal for our needs. We want to go unnoticed."

"Okay." She clapped her hands and rubbed

them together. "So what are we waiting for? Let's go."

"Are you sure you're okay? I hope I didn't overstep earlier."

"No more questions," she said, ushering him into the hallway and avoiding the subject. "We've got some cows to meet."

The safe house was basic and cheaply furnished, but it was wonderfully warm. Bryan had obviously switched on the heating prior to their arrival, before leaving the key under the mat on the porch. The journey from the cabin had taken far longer than it should have, due to the convoluted route. Brent had been concerned about being tailed so one of his deputies had followed them, a few cars behind, to ensure that nobody was tracking their movements. Then, when the deputy turned off the highway, Brent had driven the long way as an extra precaution.

Carly had been quiet in the car. She seemed to have a lot to think about, and Brent wondered if he was weighing on her mind alongside all the other issues she was dealing with. He didn't know how she truly felt about him because she refused to discuss it openly and honestly. And he had to respect her choice.

"Why don't you two go explore the place

with Uncle Amir?" Brent said to the children when seeing their disappointed faces. This new safe house wasn't quite as big as the last, and he doubted it would be well stocked with games and toys. "I think there are bunk beds upstairs."

This was enough to send Noah racing up the staircase. "I want top bunk."

Ruby chased after him, unable to keep pace. "That's not fair. I want it."

Brent held his hands up as an apology to Amir. "Sorry. I guess I walked into that one."

Amir trudged up the stairs. "I'll go be the referee."

Carly had sat on the couch and was letting her head rest on the cushion behind her, closing her eyes and retreating into her thoughts. Meanwhile, Liam was checking the perimeter of the house, probing for weak points of entry, in case they were discovered. The only thing that would help them right now was the arrest of Odell, and he seemed to be evading the police at every turn. He hadn't turned up at his usual haunts or visited his regular accomplices. The apartment where he'd been living in Casper now seemed to be abandoned. He had dropped off the radar, and Brent was now certain he was being financed by a bigger and more powerful criminal. This was a terrifying thought, as it meant that if Odell *did* manage to steal Noah and Ruby, he might have enough money to take them out of the country and start a new life. Brent simply couldn't allow that to happen.

Liam came through the front door, which led directly into the kitchen, and stood there looking both shocked and perplexed.

He held up his cell phone. "I just got a call from the forensics lab in Rock Springs. We're fortunate that the hair samples I dropped off early this morning included the roots, so they were able to extract a DNA profile really quickly. Odell's sample matches the DNA taken from the gasoline container used in the arson attack on Carly's apartment."

At the mention of her name, Carly opened her eyes and sat up straight. "It matches?"

"It sure does. The evidence proves that Odell was the arsonist."

Brent gave a little fist pump into the air. "Great. Make sure the investigating officers have all the necessary information to put on the arrest warrant." He stopped when he noticed Liam's expression. He appeared confused. "Is there something else?"

Liam came into the room and sat on a well-worn chair. "The hair sample was a mixture of two people, so both sets were analyzed."

"I must've grabbed some strands from Ruby in the tussle," Carly said. "It got tangled up with Odell's."

"That's what I figured," Liam said. "Anyway, the two hair samples yielded two full DNA profiles and you'd expect them to show a family link, right? Because Clarence Odell is supposed to be Ruby's biological father."

Brent now had to sit down too. "Are you telling me that Odell and Ruby aren't related?"

"Apparently not. Their DNA shows that they're not related at all, not even distantly."

Brent and Carly gasped in unison. This news was totally unexpected. Clarence Odell was named as the father on both birth certificates. It had never occurred to Brent that this might be a mistake or a lie.

"If Odell isn't Ruby's biological father, then he might not be Noah's father either," Carly said. "We should get him tested too."

"I agree." Liam stood up. "Is it okay if I take a mouth swab from Noah? I'll run it down to Rock Springs for an immediate analysis. They've agreed to fast-track it."

Brent didn't answer straightaway. He was still trying to absorb this stunning piece of news. If Odell wasn't the father of his foster children, then who was?

"Boss," Liam prompted. "I can use a Q-tip to take a sample and pretend it's some sort of game. It should be done without delay."

"Yeah." Brent shook himself out of his shock. "Go do it now. We need to follow this up immediately."

As Liam hurried up the stairs, Brent and Carly stared at each other in silence, before Carly finally quietly asked, "Do you think that Odell knows he's not the father?"

"Why would he go to all this trouble to snatch the children if he knows he's not their real dad? He must be in the dark about it. He assumes Noah and Ruby are his."

"But Ruby isn't his for sure," Carly said. "And I have a hunch that Noah's sample will show the same thing as his sister. The children's mother must've lied on the birth certificates."

"What do we know about her? Who was she?"

Brent had been given scant information about Noah and Ruby's birth mother, and he hadn't gone snooping. He figured that he didn't need to know. Carly now filled in those gaps.

"Linda Odell was a drug user and occasional sex worker. She married Clarence six months after Ruby was born and they lived in the town of Casper. After she died, the neighbors all said that Linda was controlled by Odell, and that she always seemed to be scared. The police ruled her death an overdose, which I don't doubt is true, but it meant that her background wasn't really investigated. So we don't know much about her life before she married Odell. The children's birth certificates state they were born in Cheyenne, so she might have a history there. I'll have to ask my boss to get an investigation started."

"An investigation?" Brent wasn't sure whether he liked where this was going. "Why?"

"Because if Clarence Odell isn't the father of Noah and Ruby, then the true father should be found. If he isn't aware he has kids, then he has a right to know."

Brent's heart dropped all the way into his stomach. He felt as though his hard-won progress was being pushed back to square one.

"These are *my* kids," he said. "I'm their true father."

Carly pinched the bridge of her nose. "I'm not trying to undermine your position as a father, Brent. I'm simply stating that the biological father has a right to be informed about the adoption of his children. The Department of Family Services has an obligation to carry out a diligent and thorough investigation to ensure that all parents are aware of their rights."

Her tone and language had turned official, as if she was in a courtroom. He was on the last leg of this process. Carly had submitted his application for approval by a judge and he could see the finish line. Until now.

"Odell's name is on the birth certificate, so let's just leave it there," he said. "We don't have to go public with the DNA results on Noah and Ruby. Nobody ever needs to know."

She eyeballed him. "Are you suggesting that we should cover this up?"

She was deliberately using inflammatory language to try to shame him. And it was working.

"It's not a cover-up," he argued. "We simply look the other way to serve the best interests of the children."

She spoke quietly and calmly. "The best interests of the children are served by finding out where they came from."

He shook his head and stood up to pace the room. A sense of panic descended, as he thought of being denied his dream of fatherhood right at the last hurdle. He had waited so long and worked so hard to come this far. Now Carly was standing in his way. Again!

"I might've known you wouldn't be on my

side," he said. "You haven't been on my side throughout this whole process."

"I'm never on the side of a parent." She was being firm with him now. "I'm only ever on the side of the child, and if you have a problem with that, I suggest you find yourself another adoption caseworker."

He sat down heavily and rested his face in his cupped hands. She had given him a well-deserved rebuke. Carly worked tirelessly to ensure that children's needs were given priority, and his children were no different. She put them first always. He would have to accept this situation and find a way through it. If he had to start the process all over again, he would do it. If he had to fight in court, he would do it. If he had to track down Noah and Ruby's father to ask him to relinquish his rights, he would do it.

He would do whatever it took to finish the job. He just hoped that Carly would be there with him to the end.

NINE

The only thing Carly could do was immerse herself in her work. This took her mind off Brent's anguish at finding out that Odell was not the children's biological father, despite being named as such on their birth certificates. She totally understood why Brent's initial reaction was to try to push forward with the final hearing and complete the adoption process, but this could come back to bite him later. They currently didn't know the situation of the biological father. If the children's mother had left him and disappeared with the kids, a judge might be sympathetic to his plight, especially if he had been searching for his missing children ever since. The father might seek to establish paternity of Noah and Ruby and overturn the adoption ruling. Cases like this were incredibly rare, and adoptions were seldom overturned, but it made sense to face these problems before proceeding. She wanted to avoid entering a legal minefield.

Having worked on several assignments in her caseload, she began to check her emails before breaking for lunch. That's when she saw a message from the courthouse in Cheyenne. An emergency hearing had been organized for the following day regarding the Buchannan case. It appeared that Kendall Buchannan's situation had changed and he was applying for a sudden delay to the family court proceedings. No further details were given on the email, but a sense of anger rose in the pit of her stomach. Zoe Buchannan would be worried and scared to know that her ex-husband was playing the system in order to buy himself some time. His application for visitation rights was not looking good and this most recent request was certainly a cynical ploy to halt Carly's momentum in terminating his parental responsibilities.

Navigating through her folders on her laptop, she opened up the Buchannan file and began preparing a report for the judge, in which she would request that this application be denied. She would have to present it in person, which meant another journey to Cheyenne, except this time she hoped it would not be as dangerous as the last.

As the time ticked by, she didn't notice how late it was getting until her stomach began to rumble. Then Brent knocked at her bedroom door and poked his head around it. She was sitting cross-legged on her bed with her laptop balanced on her knees, which wasn't an ideal office environment, but this new safe house didn't offer much space.

"It's getting late," he said. "I'm starting on dinner and I wondered whether you had any food preferences for this evening."

She checked her watch. "Oh goodness! I worked right through lunch." She closed the lid of her computer. "I'll come help." She swung her legs off the bed and sat there for a second, noticing Brent's pale complexion. "Did you manage to find any information about Noah and Ruby's mother today?"

"I found records of Linda Odell giving birth to Noah and Ruby at the same Cheyenne hospital," he replied. "She gave both children the surname Vaughan, which was also her name at the time. On their birth certificates, the section that identifies the father was left blank. Linda married Clarence Odell in Casper when Ruby was six months old and Noah was two and a half. She then changed their surnames to Odell and added Clarence as the father on their birth certificates. From what I learned today, this would've been an easy thing to do because they were married. Married men are always assumed to be the father of any children in the marriage."

"That's right," she confirmed. "Nobody would've questioned it or asked for a paternity test. But Linda couldn't have amended the certificates without her husband's agreement, so there's still a chance that Clarence Odell believed he was the father. We need to find out where Linda was living when the children were born and whether Odell was on the scene."

"I managed to trace a couple people who knew Linda in Casper and I called them today. They confirmed that Linda and Clarence lived in a dilapidated house in the downtown area, but they weren't able to give me any information on her life before marrying Odell. That information is a little trickier to uncover. I've got Liam working on it right now."

Carly smiled. "I'm really proud of the way you're dealing with this situation, Brent. The news about Noah and Ruby's biological father obviously came as a huge shock, but you're trying to do the right thing and play it by the book. I know that must be hard."

He came into the room and sat on the bed

beside her. "It's the hardest thing I've ever had to do. I want to pretend that this guy doesn't exist. I want him to go away and leave us alone, which is crazy because I've never even met him. I shouldn't make assumptions about him. He might be a high court judge or a human rights lawyer, for all I know."

Carly bumped her shoulder into his. "Linda Odell didn't mix in those kinds of circles, so I think you're letting your imagination run away with you."

He sighed. "I guess so." He angled his body toward hers and his beautiful hazel eyes settled on her face. "What would happen if I located Noah and Ruby's father and he wanted to see them? Or worse still, if he wanted custody?"

Carly had been expecting these questions to come but they still tugged at her heartstrings nonetheless. Brent had been a father to his foster children for almost a year and they loved him as much as he loved them. In an ideal world, the adoption would be simple and straightforward, and they would live happily ever after. But this wasn't a fairy tale. It was real life, with all its messy complications.

"Every case is decided on its own merits," she replied. "It's highly unlikely that a judge would decide to remove Noah and Ruby from a stable and loving home, so the risk of you losing them is incredibly low."

"But it's not as low as zero?"

She took his hand. "Don't try to predict what might happen, because you'll only imagine the very worst scenarios in your head."

His eyes continued to rest on her face. "The worst scenario I can imagine is losing the children and you as well."

She said nothing for a while. She wanted to tell him that she also dreaded the time when they wouldn't see each other anymore. In spite of her determination to keep an emotional distance, she'd only ended up caring about him even more. Since confiding in him about Laurie, he had counseled and comforted her. He also prayed for her and regularly passed along pieces of Scripture to help restore her faith. Slowly, she was shedding all of the negative feelings that had been a burden on her back.

"You won't lose the children, Brent," she said, choosing not to address his concern about losing her too. "Whatever happens next, I'll be here to advise you. I'll stand up in court and vouch for you. You've been there for me recently so let me repay the favor. I'll be with you every step of the way."

"Do you mean that?"

"I mean it," she said. "I'm by your side."

He leaned forward and planted a light and feathery kiss on her lips, so fleeting that she almost didn't register it. Her heart skipped and she jolted a little, as if she had touched a live wire.

"Thank you," he said, standing up to leave. "If I can do anything for you in return, let me know."

"You protect me from Odell every day. You don't owe me more than that."

He stopped at the door, turned and smiled. "What I owe you can't be put into words."

As always, dinnertime was a messy and loud affair. While Carly, Brent, Noah, Ruby and Liam sat around the kitchen table, Amir sat out on the porch, keeping watch. Brent had also installed two cameras on the sides of the house, giving them an all-round view. If motion was detected by the cameras, an alarm would sound on Brent's cell and he could spring into action.

"Hot lettuce is yucky," Ruby said, holding a piece of it between her fingers as if it were a worm. "I don't want it."

"It's called cabbage," Noah said, making a face in apparent solidarity. "It comes in purple too but all cabbage is gross, whatever the color."

Brent pointed a finger at Noah in admonishment. One of his dinner table rules was to never use the word *gross* to describe food. Otherwise, Ruby would use it constantly as a way of avoiding eating anything that wasn't sweet.

"Just eat a little bit," he coaxed. "It's full of vitamins."

Ruby let out a small scream and pushed her plate away. "Cooties!"

Brent couldn't help laughing, despite trying very hard to stop himself. "Vitamins aren't bugs, Ruby. They're good for you. They make you grow big and strong."

Noah reached up to Brent's bicep and poked it. "Like you, Daddy?"

His emotional reaction was immediate and strong, as his eyes became hot. This was the very first time that Noah had called him Daddy. After the terrible day he'd had attempting to track down the children's birth father, this one little word made all the problems melt away.

"Yep," he said, keeping his response short because he was choked up. "Just like me."

Noah stabbed a piece of cabbage with his fork and shoved it in his mouth. He clearly didn't like the taste but chewed and swallowed it anyway. Meanwhile, Carly watched with a smile on her face, seeming to enjoy the interaction. Her decision to remain childless made no sense to Brent. She clearly reveled in their family time and came alive when playing with the children. She was depriving herself of so much joy because of her determination to stay single forever.

Reminding himself that Carly's life choices were none of his business, he concentrated on their meal, encouraging Ruby to eat a little of everything on her plate. With a lot of cajoling and distraction, he managed to get her to eat almost everything, and Noah did the same. After everybody was finished, Liam offered to run a bath for Ruby, which prompted a peal of excitement from her because she had spotted sparkly bubble bath on the side of the tub earlier in the day. She jumped up and ran to the stairs, eager to try it out.

"I'll go play upstairs," Noah said as he followed his sister and Uncle Liam. "And when it's my turn in the tub I do *not* want sparkles."

"That's okay. You can have fresh water all of your own," Brent called as he watched them disappear up the stairs. "But I'll come up there to make sure you wash behind your ears."

"Your family is wonderful, Brent," Carly

said, gathering the dishes into a pile. "You're truly blessed."

He went to the dishwasher and started to load it. "I know. Did you notice how Noah called me Daddy just now?" He felt himself getting choked up again. "It just tripped off his tongue."

"Of course I noticed." She gave him a playful punch on his arm. "He also wants to be big and strong like you. Boys need a daddy as a role model, and you're giving him a great example of manhood."

Brent put down the plate he was holding. "Kids also need a mommy. I just wish I could offer them that too."

Carly leaned against the sink next to him. "I wish that every child could have a mother and a father who loved them and took care of them, but things don't always work out that way. Sometimes, we have to do our best with what we're given. There are no perfect parents or perfect families." She cast her gaze down to the floor. "And sometimes the parents who seem to have no faults are the ones who have the darkest secrets."

He guessed she was talking about Oliver Dowd, and he gave her shoulder a reassuring squeeze. He wanted to hold her but thought he shouldn't, especially after kissing her earlier. He resolved to be more careful about overstepping.

"You know something?" she said. "I haven't thought about Laurie all day, not until this moment. She's usually the first person on my mind when I wake up, but I've been thinking about her less and less lately." Her brow wrinkled beneath her blond bangs. "I'm not sure whether that's a good or bad thing."

"It's a good thing," he said. "I know you think you should pay some kind of penance for what happened, but you deserve to move on with your life."

She nodded, as if she was finally starting to believe him. "Talking to you about it really helped me to understand my feelings. I hadn't realized I was so angry. I was angry with Oliver Dowd, with God and with myself. Anger is such a destructive emotion."

"Trust me, I know. Anyone who works in law enforcement is all too aware of what anger can do."

She turned to him and opened her mouth as if she wanted to ask a question but then thought better of it.

"Ask me anything," he prompted. "I'll answer honestly."

"Why didn't you rage against God when your wife died?"

He sat down on a chair to give a considered and measured response. This wasn't the question he had been expecting her to ask. Brent had been left devastated by the loss of Tamsin, but he had never thought to blame God or direct any fury toward Him. Quite the opposite had happened. God had been his refuge and his fortress, soothing his pain and giving him hope. God had slowly turned the darkness into light, and Brent's love for Him had burgeoned because of it.

"You just mentioned that there are no perfect parents," he said. "But that's not true. God is a perfect Father, and He's always given me what I need throughout my life. It didn't occur to me to be angry with Him after Tamsin died, because He is the only perfect thing in an imperfect world." He looked up at her. "Does that make sense?"

She gazed at him. "Totally."

"Good."

He stood up to begin stacking the pans into the dishwasher, while she watched him silently.

"What else do you want to know?" he asked, with a smile. "Because it's obvious that you're not done with the questions."

"Do you think that I could maybe come to your church sometime? If it's okay with you?

I haven't been to a service in a while, so I'm a little out of practice."

His smile grew wider. "As soon as this is all over, I'd be honored to take you to a family service and introduce you to everybody." He laughed. "But you need to be forewarned that Ruby might sign you up for Sunday school duty."

"That's okay. You know I'm good with kids."

"Great. It's a date."

He turned his attention back to cleaning up the kitchen. Carly couldn't possibly be a better match for him, and he wished with all his heart that things were different. If she weren't his adoption caseworker, or so dedicated to her job, they could easily fall madly in love. But in an imperfect world, he would have to settle for being her friend.

Carly wanted to shout and bang the table in the family court in Cheyenne. The judge had allowed Kendall Buchannan to manipulate him into delaying the proceedings regarding visitation rights of his ten-month-old baby boy. As the murder charge against him had been dropped, Buchannan had successfully argued that he required time to present a new case to the court, one which would give a full and glowing picture of his new circumstances.

"Your Honor," Carly said, maintaining a calm exterior. "Child Protective Services does not believe this man should be given any type of access to his baby. He is a flight risk. I strongly suspect he will abscond with the child if given the opportunity."

"Ms. Engelman," the judge said, looking at her atop his glasses from his bench. "Mr. Buchannan is wearing an ankle tag. If he plans on absconding, then he'd be very easy to find."

"The tag is due to be removed later today," Carly said dryly. "This information is in the new paperwork submitted by Kendall Buchannan to the court yesterday."

"Ah!" The judge pretended to scan his papers. "I see. Well, that's a good sign, isn't it? It means that the police see no reason to continue to monitor his movements."

Carly sighed inwardly. "His tag is being removed because the murder charge against him has been dropped by the State of Wyoming, but that doesn't mean he no longer represents a danger to his wife and child." She looked down at Zoe Buchannan, who stared straight ahead, resolutely avoiding the gaze of Kendall, who sat at a table to their left. "May

I remind you that Mrs. Buchannan has not only accused her husband of domestic abuse but was also due to be a witness for the prosecution in his trial. He harbors deep resentment toward her."

Kendall Buchannan was staring at Carly with cold eyes, and she guessed that Zoe was not the only woman he despised. She tried to ignore his obvious hatred for her, but it was no easy feat to overlook a man of his size, six foot three and around two hundred and fifty pounds of pure muscle.

"Unfortunately, many divorces are acrimonious," the judge said, looking between Mr. and Mrs. Buchannan. "And my job is to uphold values of fairness in deciding what is in the best interests of any children arising from the marriage."

"The best outcome for the child in this instance is to remain with his mother. I recommend that you award full custody to Zoe Buchannan and terminate the rights of the father."

"Yes, thank you, Ms. Engelman." The judge was irritated with her. "I must admit I was leaning in that direction until now, but circumstances have changed. Mr. Buchannan is no longer facing a murder charge, which would suggest that he is innocent. An innocent man should not be punished by losing access to his child."

"He is *not* innocent, Your Honor. Every single trial witness, except Mrs. Buchannan, withdrew their cooperation from trial proceedings, leading to a collapse in the case. The police suspect they were either subjected to intimidation tactics or paid off."

The judge turned his attention to Kendall. "Do you have anything to say about this, Mr. Buchannan?"

"Yes, Your Honor." Kendall stood up. He was sharply dressed in a black suit and wearing a gleaming Rolex watch. He had also surprisingly chosen to represent himself rather than hire an attorney, which spoke volumes about his arrogance. "I am a simple man with nothing to hide, and I'm truly grateful to the FBI for uncovering discrepancies in the inaccurate witness testimonies, which is why the flawed case against me collapsed."

He side-eyed Carly with a smug smile and she flared her nostrils in disgust. Kendall Buchannan was an educated man with razor-sharp intelligence. When this intellect was combined with a ruthless criminal streak, he became one of the most dangerous men in the state. He ran drug gangs in all major towns and cities across Wyoming and had amassed a personal fortune of tens of millions of dollars, which he had funneled into South American properties and banks.

"I love my son," Kendall continued with a hand across his heart. "I would never hurt him or run away with him. I haven't seen him since he was tiny, and I miss him terribly. My wife took off and abandoned me shortly after he was born, telling lies to the police about my alleged criminal activities and supposed violent tendencies. She told these lies because she wants to prevent my son from knowing his father. And that isn't fair, sir. I'm asking you to see me as a human being rather than the monster that my wife portrays."

Carly shook her head, feeling as though Kendall really should be given a round of applause for that performance. His eloquence, however, was having an effect on the judge, who looked on with sympathy.

"I am inclined to consider permitting Mr. Buchannan supervised visitation rights," he said. "This would allow professionals to monitor how the child and his father interact."

Carly couldn't prevent a shout from escaping her mouth. "No!"

"I would be overjoyed to see my son in a supervised capacity, Your Honor," Kendall said. "Just tell me when and where."

As Zoe began to cry beside her, Carly knew she had to make a passionate plea on behalf of the mother and child. This was why she could never entertain a life with Brent. She was needed as an advocate for those who did not have a strong voice of their own.

"Please, Your Honor," she said, clasping her hands in a pleading motion. "Don't make any rash decisions. I know from personal experience that children's lives can be placed in certain danger when we throw caution to the wind. Kendall Buchannan is a well-known drug lord in this state and he's feared by everyone who knows him. His wife remains under police protection in a secure location because they believe her life is at risk. He has amassed an eye-watering personal fortune from his criminal activities, which would allow him to move south of the border and live in luxury, far away from the reach of American justice. Don't give him the chance to take his son with him."

Kendall stood up. "This is a joke, Your Honor. I'm a property developer who abides by the law. These allegations from Ms. Engelman are all unproven lies. I'm innocent until proven guilty, right?"

"Don't take the risk, Your Honor," Carly implored. "He's a con man."

The judge tapped his chin. "But supervised access would ensure the child's safety, surely?"

"No, it wouldn't," she shot back. "This man has no respect for the law. He would steal his son and shoot anyone who stands in his way."

Kendall held up his hands. "I don't even own a gun, sir."

Zoe now rose from her seat and pointed at him, her face streaked with tears. "You have enough guns to start your own war."

"Let's all settle down." The judge banged on the bench. "I've heard enough to make an interim judgment."

Carly waited with her heart in her mouth.

"Mr. and Mrs. Buchannan's baby son, Jordan, will remain in the full custody of his mother," the judge said. "No visitation rights will be awarded to the father until I can be satisfied of his character and his intentions. I will agree to Mr. Buchannan's request for a delay to a final and permanent decision regarding custody. We will meet again once I've received Mr. Buchannan's written report. Thank you for your time today."

As the judge stood to leave the family court, Zoe grabbed hold of Carly and pulled her close.

"Thank you," she whispered. "Thank you for keeping my son safe."

Carly patted her back. "It's why I do this job."

As she picked up her briefcase, a police officer stood close by, waiting to escort Zoe from the building, and Kendall sat with his lips pursed in anger. Carly couldn't wait to return to Brent and let the stresses of the day melt away. She knew he would be just outside the courthouse, pacing the ground, ready to greet her with a beaming smile.

It was with a jolt of surprise that she realized she might love him. And that was not what she had planned for her life. This was a problem she had not anticipated.

Carly was upbeat when she emerged from family court, pleased about how the session had gone. Yet she was eager to put some personal space between her and Brent, ensuring they remained a good distance apart, not even brushing against each other as they walked to the car. She was wearing black trousers and a blue blouse, which was the most formal outfit she currently owned. She had complained of feeling dowdy and underdressed that morning, so Ruby had given her some costume jewelry from her box. Brent had expected Carly to politely decline it, but she had pinned a pink flower brooch to her blouse and clipped some diamante earrings to her lobes. As Ruby had danced around the kitchen, admiring how pretty Carly looked, Brent had found himself loving her more than ever. She always took the time to truly listen to the children and take notice of their thoughts and opinions. She even wore kitsch jewelry to family court because a little girl told her she looked like a princess.

"Do you want to stop off at a restaurant on the way back?" Brent asked, standing in the sunny parking lot and checking the vicinity for signs of danger. "Are you hungry?"

"Let's get back as soon as possible," she replied. "I can pick up a sandwich when we stop for gas."

He was disappointed. He had been looking forward to spending some time alone with her, talking about anything and everything under the sun. But he should've remembered what happened last time they'd taken a trip to Cheyenne. Carly was most likely being super-cautious. Or she was avoiding spending time with him. Her feelings toward him were impossible to read at the best of times, and this afternoon she seemed to be especially distant.

"Let me check the car," he said, encouraging her to stand well back in the lot. "Somebody might've attached a tracker to it while we were gone."

He got down on his knees and peered underneath, feeling with his hands around the wheel wells and hubcaps. The vehicle showed no signs of forced entry so a device couldn't have been placed inside. Sticking two fingers into the tailpipe, he came into contact with something that shouldn't be there, something that was small but hard. With his fingernails he scrabbled his way around, touching wires, plastic and tape, which were the unmistakable signs of a homemade explosive device.

He stood up sharply, just managing to call out a warning to Carly before he was lifted off his feet and hurled through the air amid a flash of orange and yellow. He was slammed against the ground with the force of a freight train.

Then the pain set in.

TEN

The parking lot was filled with noise, as car alarms screeched and people screamed. Brent turned over onto his back, holding his elbow where it had scraped hard on the ground and flayed the skin. He was woozy and disoriented, and his ears rang with a high-pitched tone. While trying to regulate his breathing, a man loomed over him, wearing a black security uniform. Brent recognized him as an employee of the courthouse.

"Are you okay?" the man asked. "What happened here?"

"Bomb," Brent croaked from his lying position. "Where is the woman who was with me?"

The guard looked around. "The blond woman who was attending the family court session today?"

"That's the one."

He shook his head. "I don't see her."

With a huge exhalation of pain, Brent pushed himself to his knees, before the guard gave him a helping hand and hauled him to his feet. He had no broken bones, but he hurt like crazy all over his body, even his toenails.

"I gotta find her. She's in danger."

"We're all in danger," the security guard said. "That's why we need to get into the courthouse immediately."

While clutching his bleeding elbow, Brent began to stagger around the burning car, which emitted a heat that stung his face. The tailpipe bomb had been small but the damage it caused was immense. Nobody inside this vehicle would have escaped with their life.

"Carly!" he yelled. "Where are you?"

"She might be inside," the guard said. "We started getting everybody into the lobby when the car burst into flames." He put an arm around Brent and ushered him. "Let's go, buddy. The police and fire department are on their way. We need to clear the area."

"Carly!" Brent yelled once more as they made their way inside. "I'll find you."

Against a backdrop of mayhem, he entered the courthouse to begin his search there.

The interior of the courthouse was teeming with people, and Carly had been pushed to the back of the lobby by the throng. The building was large, with multiple courts, all of which seemed to be in use that day. The explosion had been so loud that the guard who had helped her to safety told her he'd felt the walls shake. The inhabitants of the courts had, of course, come streaming from their rooms to see what was going on.

Thankfully, Brent had been able to shout a warning to Carly before the danger hit. She had already begun to run away when the car became a fireball. The blast had knocked her from her feet and sent her sprawling on the asphalt, but other than a hole in the knee of her pants, she was unscathed. A security guard had scooped her up and ushered her inside before she'd had the opportunity to look for Brent.

And now she was alone, trying to fight her way forward to find him. But it was proving impossible, due to the chaos and panic around her. Security guards were attempting to shout above the noise, imploring people to remain calm, but the rumor of a terrorist attack was being openly discussed. Why else would a car bomb be detonated in a courthouse parking lot? Of course, the public didn't have the benefit of Carly's knowledge and likely wouldn't listen anyway.

As she pressed her back against the wall in an attempt to skirt around the edges toward the exit, she saw him. Not Brent, but Odell. He was wearing a shirt and tie in an apparent attempt to blend in, but his stringy hair and gaunt face were impossible to disguise. Their eyes locked together for a few seconds. He was only a few feet away, but they were separated by a crowd of tightly packed people.

He seemed to be formulating a plan of attack while she sought a route of escape. In this mayhem, it was likely that nobody would notice a knife being stuck into her side, or her screams mingling with the others. She wasn't safe there. She had to run. Turning on her heel, she raced for the stairs, where the guard had left his post. She gripped the rail for support as she took the steps two at a time. She thought she heard her name being yelled, but she didn't look back. She had to find somewhere to hide. Her purse was on the asphalt outside, dropped there when she was thrown to the ground. And inside that purse were her cell phone and gun. Guns were always checked at reception at the courthouse, but in this situation, the guards were unable to implement normal procedures. Odell could be armed.

Reaching the second floor, she was faced

with a corridor of doors, some open, others closed. Running along the carpet, she sought to locate a hiding spot that wouldn't be too obvious. If she was able to lock a door once she was inside, that would almost certainly be a dead giveaway to her presence. These rooms all seemed to be administrative offices, filled with desks and filing cabinets, but completely devoid of people. She opened each closed door, checking behind the handle to see if a key rested in a lock on the inside. Meanwhile, she knew that her time was running out. Once Odell had fought his way through the mass of people, he would be hot on her heels.

Finally, she found a key and pulled it from the lock. Then, while she remained in the corridor, she closed the door and locked it, pocketing the key in her pants. Then she ran to a janitor's closet at the end of the corridor, quickly slipping inside and leaning against the door. Her heart banged like a drum in a darkness that smelled of floor polish. Within a few seconds, she heard heavy footsteps in the corridor. Odell was running from room to room, seeking her out. She heard desks being tipped and computers crashing to the ground. These sounds mingled with the shouts and cries of the crowd downstairs and the sirens that were heading their way.

Eventually, Odell found the locked room and took the bait. He began to kick the door over and over in an attempt to break it down. The door apparently held firm. Would his failure to access the room buy her enough time? Surely, once the police were on-site, they would sweep the building for security reasons. All she needed was another few minutes.

Yet time was not on her side. The locked door seemed to fly open with a loud bang and sounds of moving furniture and falling cabinets reached Carly's ears. She grabbed the first thing within reach: a mop. Yanking off the head, she held the stick in her hands, wondering if she could use the element of surprise to her advantage. Was it better to jump out now? Or wait to be discovered?

She waited. And waited. But she could hear Odell no longer. The distant sirens had now reached the building, and even though her tiny hiding place had no windows, she guessed that a crowd of uniformed firefighters and police officers would now be in the lot, extinguishing the flames and bringing calmness to the panic. The handle of the door behind her turned. She felt it slowly scrape against her back. Turning around, she threw open the door and lunged with the stick. On the other side of the janitor's closet, Brent caught the wood with a swift flick of his hand, closing his fist around the makeshift weapon and stopping it dead. She stared at him in surprise. He was dirty and bloodied, with a torn sweatshirt sleeve and a scraped elbow. But she had never seen him looking so handsome.

"Oh, Brent!" she exclaimed, falling into his arms. "I'm so glad to see you."

He squeezed her tight. "I don't know about you, but I'm really beginning to dislike the city."

Carly wet a cloth in the bowl of antiseptic liquid and dabbed it gently onto Brent's elbow. He winced in pain and gritted his teeth as she removed all the dirt from the wound, making sure to leave no trace behind. Brent had refused an assessment from paramedics, as he'd wanted to return to Noah and Ruby without delay. And Carly had agreed with him because, much to her surprise, a maternal instinct had been sparked in her. She was now fiercely protective of those children and didn't want to be out of their sight for long. This must be how it felt to be a mother, and it was a yearning that she had never thought she'd experience.

After giving the police a brief overview of what happened, Brent had sourced a car from a Cheyenne rentals firm, and they'd left the city as soon as possible. Both he and Carly had promised to supply statements via email, after which an investigation would begin to find evidence that would hopefully link Odell to the bomb.

"How did Odell find you today?" Brent asked. "Would he have been able to access the court schedule for the day?"

"Absolutely not." She dried his wound with a soft cloth. "Family court sessions are private and not open to the public. Besides, there's been an extra layer of secrecy for the Buchannan custody case because the FBI didn't want rival drug gangs turning up to attack Kendall. Today's hearing wouldn't have fully appeared on any court calendar, even in official circles. The names would have been redacted."

"So how did Odell know about it?"

Carly had been wondering the same thing herself. "I really don't know."

"What about this Kendall Buchannan guy? Could he have passed along the information to Odell? He sounds like a shady character."

Carly remembered the way Kendall Buchannan's eyes had bored into her with such undisguised hatred.

"That's possible. If Buchannan knows that Odell wants me dead, then he'd definitely give him details of my whereabouts."

Brent held his arm straight in the air as Carly wound a bandage around the injury.

"Does Buchannan hate you enough to bankroll Odell?" he asked. "Because we already figured out that somebody is picking up Odell's tab."

Carly stopped what she was doing. This made a lot of sense.

"Yeah. Currently, I'm the only person standing in the way of Buchannan getting visitation rights to his son, so he'd sure like to see me dead. And he'd be able to keep his hands clean by paying somebody else to do it."

"But if you were killed, another employee of the CPS would take over the custody case, right? It wouldn't nix it."

She tied the ends of the bandage together to secure it. "I know this case inside out and I know how to handle the judge. Nobody is a better advocate for Zoe Buchannan than me. A new caseworker would be a gift to Kendall Buchannan right now."

"Okay." He bent his elbow and then straightened his arm, testing the bandage. "Then I think it's safe to presume that Buchannan is a part of our problem."

"Oh boy, ain't that the truth." This came from Amir, who descended the stairs with a cell phone in one hand and a handful of scribbled notes in the other. "I just got off the phone with the chief of police in Cheyenne. An informant has come forward tonight with information that you'll want to hear, boss. It might come as a shock."

Brent rubbed his forehead with thumb and forefinger. "Hit me with it, Deputy Faisal. I don't think anything can faze me anymore."

Brent soon found out that his words would ring hollow, because he sat in stunned silence after Amir told him the news.

"You can't be serious. Kendall Buchannan is the biological father of Noah and Ruby?" He was glad that the children were tucked up in bed, well out of earshot. "How? What? Really?"

Carly's hand came to rest on his shoulder and squeezed. He felt that she truly understood the devastating impact of this revelation. They had become a team.

"Linda Odell used to be the partner of Kendall Buchannan in Cheyenne," Amir said, reading from his notes. "She gave birth to

Noah and Ruby while they were together, but she left shortly after Ruby's birth. By all accounts, Kendall got her hooked on drugs and was violent toward her."

"That sounds like him," Carly said. "Women and children are his property in his book."

Amir continued the story. "When Linda vanished, Kendall hired a bunch of private investigators to find her, but she was smart. She stopped using her bank accounts and she didn't update any official documents with a new address. Kendall assumed she'd gone out of state but she actually only moved to Casper, just one hundred and eighty miles away. She was right under his nose and he didn't have a clue."

"We know she then married Odell," Brent said. "And added his name to the birth certificates."

Amir nodded. "That's right, but Buchannan was oblivious to this. Linda even planted false evidence by applying for a new driver's license in California, so that's where Buchannan was focused in his search. He was furious about having his children stolen from him. According to the informant, he's never stopped looking for them and he's determined to get them back by any means necessary. He's now using Odell to snatch them."

"How did he find out where the kids were?" Carly asked. "Did Odell tell him?"

"Now, this is where you might get mad, boss," Amir said to Brent. "Because it's tough to hear."

Brent gritted his teeth. "Tell me."

Amir took a deep breath. "After Linda died and the children were fostered by you and Tamsin, Odell got in touch with Buchannan to make a deal. He explained that Linda had declared him as the legal father of Noah and Ruby, and that he would try to gain custody of them through the court. Once the kids were his, he'd planned to sell them to their biological father."

Brent stood up, anger bubbling inside. "He wanted to *sell* them? Like old furniture in a yard sale? I don't have the words."

"Kendall immediately agreed to a purchase price of half a million dollars per child," Amir continued. "He was already facing a murder charge at this point. He was also fighting his wife for access to his baby son, so Odell was his best hope of ever getting Noah and Ruby back. Kendall thinks that Child Protective Services is out to get him, but he especially hates Carly because she's a constant problem."

"I stopped Odell from gaining custody

of Noah and Ruby," she said. "And now I'm stopping Buchannan from seeing his baby son. I'm the one person who's preventing him from gaining access to all of his children, so it's no surprise that he hates me."

"Odell has been acting on Buchannan's orders ever since he set fire to your apartment," Amir said. "We assumed that Odell was taking revenge for the loss of his kids, but that's not true. It's Buchannan who wants you dead. He's desperate for another caseworker to be allocated to the custody battle with his wife because he thinks you're too good at your job. All he needs is for a judge to grant him one visit with his son and he's all set."

"All set for what?" Carly didn't know whether she wanted to hear the answer.

"To steal his baby by force and then leave the country. He's got a luxury villa in Nicaragua, where he plans to take the children. He wants all three of them to be raised by him there."

Brent stood by the window, staring at the field of cows as his mind raced to catch up. This was a lot to take in. He just needed to be absolutely sure that this information was reliable.

"Who is the informant and why has he come forward now?"

"His identity is confidential, but he's one of Buchannan's drug runners," Amir replied. "He assumed his boss was going to prison for murder, so he helped himself to a chunk of the profits while Buchannan was busy dealing with other matters. Now that the murder charge has been dropped and Buchannan's electronic tag is removed, the informant is in big trouble. He approached the FBI to ask for protection in return for cooperation on all of Buchannan's criminal activities. The Bureau is currently arranging to get him into a witness protection program while they build a case."

"How do we know that the informant is telling the truth about Buchannan being the biological parent?" Brent was clutching at straws because he didn't want it to be true. "It could be a ruse."

"Buchannan's DNA is on file," Amir said. "It's been compared with Ruby's and Noah's DNA. It's been confirmed that there is a genetic father match on both children."

Brent winced as the word *father* was used yet again to describe Buchannan. Carly obviously saw his expression and went to him, placing a reassuring hand on his forearm.

"Right now, Noah and Ruby need their *real* father to take care of them," she said. "The role of a father goes way beyond genetics, and you're the most loyal and protective dad I've ever known. Buchannan has no right to call himself anything other than a stranger to Noah and Ruby."

"Thank you," he said quietly. "That means a lot."

"This situation just got a whole lot more complicated," Amir said. "Until now, we thought we were dealing with a petty criminal with an axe to grind, but now we know that we're facing a powerful drug lord with unlimited money."

"And his electronic tag just got removed," Brent said. "So he can move around freely."

"Yes, he can, which is why the FBI thinks you should place Noah and Ruby in protective custody until he's caught. With the informant's new evidence, Buchannan will be arrested and charged with offenses of drug trafficking, money laundering and seeking to transport children illegally from the country. They're all federal crimes."

Brent sat down and placed his head in his hands. He had assumed he was capable of shielding his children from danger, but the threat had just escalated beyond his wildest imagination. Buchannan was violent, determined and ruthless. And his movements were no longer being monitored, so he was as free as a bird.

"Where is the nearest FBI office?" he asked Amir.

"The closest is in Casper. It's a four-hour drive from here."

Brent made an immediate decision. "We'll leave early in the morning and go to Casper. The kids are fast asleep and I don't want to scare them by waking them up and bundling them in a car. Besides, I think we're safe here for the time being. Nobody except my pastor is aware of our location, and we can trust him. Let's all get a good night's sleep and be ready at seven in the morning."

"I think that's a sensible choice, Brent," Carly said. "The FBI will add an extra layer of security to the one you already have in place."

He smiled at her. She was being so kind and compassionate, going to extra lengths to let him know he was being a strong and caring father. He loved her for doing this. In fact, he loved her for plenty of reasons, but he couldn't act on any of those feelings in the current moment. Perhaps he would never be able to let her know how strongly he felt. He could only take each day as it came and hope that they made it through this danger alive.

After that, anything was possible.

* * *

Carly packed a suitcase for the third time, watching the clock turn to midnight. Learning that Kendall Buchannan was the biological father of Noah and Ruby had shaken Brent to the core. When Odell had been fighting through the courts for custody of the children, Carly had kept Brent and Tamsin updated every step of the way. They couldn't make an application to adopt the children until the biological father's rights had been terminated. So when Carly gave them the news that Clarence Odell had lost his case, they thought that all barriers had been removed. They made their application the very same day.

Sitting on the bed, Carly cast her mind back to the time when Brent and Tamsin had signed the adoption application papers and handed them to her. Little did she know at the time that within four weeks, Tamsin would have tragically passed away. Even more difficult for Carly to believe was the fact that she would subsequently fall in love with Brent and grow close to his children. It wasn't what she had expected to happen.

This whole experience had given her much to think about, particularly in regard to her decision to remain childless. While she was still committed to the children that she safeguarded in her job, she was now yearning to be a mother. The recent time she had spent with Noah and Ruby had shown her exactly how much love she could offer a child of her own. She needn't even get married. She was considering adopting one of the many children languishing in the care system. Thousands of children across the country needed loving homes, and she would be able to provide one. It would require some careful planning to juggle her job and motherhood, but it was certainly feasible.

A small voice worked its way into her head: *But you love Brent?*

She let out a long sigh, wrestling with these feelings. Brent already had a complete family of his own, one which he had formed with his wife. Carly had no right to barge her way into it and stake a claim. Brent might not want to adopt another child, whereas Carly was certain that she wished to offer a child a safe haven in which to grow and thrive. It was better not to lead him on, but to forge her own path and build her own family.

She heard a squeak outside her door that sounded like a foot stepping on one of the creaky boards.

"Hello?" she called. "Who's there?"

The door opened and Brent stood in the

doorway. "Don't panic. It's only me. I saw that your light was on and I wondered if everything was okay."

"Yeah." She zipped her suitcase closed. "I just wanted to get everything ready for tomorrow, so that I don't make us late." She smiled, tightening the cord on the bathrobe she wore over her pajamas. "I'm not a morning person."

He laughed. "It's a good thing you don't have children because they are most *definitely* morning people."

"Actually, I've been thinking a lot about having a child lately. Being here with you and the kids has made me reassess my priorities."

He looked pleasantly surprised. "Really?"

"Yeah. I'd like a family of my own. I could adopt a child and adapt my life to fit around him or her."

"Oh." He now seemed disappointed. "You're thinking of going it alone, huh?"

"Why not? It's better for a child to be part of a single parent family rather than growing up in the care system, right? I know the ideal scenario is for children to have a mom and a dad, but life doesn't always work that way."

"In an ideal world, Noah and Ruby would have both a mom and a dad, but I guess you're right. Life doesn't always work out that way."

"You'll find someone in the future," she said, avoiding his eyes. "A man like you won't stay single forever."

"What about you?" He rubbed the back of his neck as if he was experiencing a sudden bout of shyness. "Do you see somebody in your future?"

"I don't think so. I've been single for my entire life. I'm probably too old and set in my ways."

"You're never too old to fall in love."

She finally met his eyes, expecting him to be smiling, but he was serious and somber, as if this was no laughing matter. His eyes were full of emotion, and she didn't know how to respond. So she changed the subject.

"I'll file a court application to reject any possible claims from Kendall Buchannan relating to paternity of Noah and Ruby. It would be wise to preempt anything he might throw at us in the future, even if he's in jail. I'm sure the court will grant the request, so we can proceed with the adoption as normal."

"That's good news. I want to tell you how much I appreciate and value your support. I'm glad we had this chance to get to know each other a little better, even if the circumstances aren't the best."

She sensed that he was holding something

back. "Me too. You've helped me deal with a lot of trauma and pain. And you showed me how to trust in the Lord again. Thank you."

"It's my pleasure." They stood in silence for a few seconds before he added, "I'll let you get some sleep. I'll wake you at six."

"Great. Good night, Brent."

"Good night."

He backed out of the door and clicked it closed, leaving her pondering all the words that she wished she had the courage to say.

The kettle whistled in the dark kitchen, and Brent turned off the burner. While adding hot water to his peppermint tea bag, he ran through his conversation with Carly, imagining all the things he could've said differently. He could've been more open with her and told her how he felt. He could've pushed her beyond her comfort zone.

But it was obvious that she wasn't prepared to take a risk on loving him. After a lifetime of being alone, she couldn't foresee happiness with somebody. It was a shame, but it was her choice. He just wished that the rejection didn't make his heart hurt quite this much.

"You'll get over it," he told himself, blowing on his tea. "Time heals everything."

In the distance, car headlights turned onto

the long lane that led to the safe house. He froze by the kitchen window, anxiety rising. He was taking the first guard shift that night so he was the first line of defense. He reasoned that this was possibly a lost traveler, making a U-turn. But it bypassed the ideal spot to turn around and the lights came closer, as the car drove slowly and purposefully toward the house.

He grabbed his radio from the counter. "Code Red outside," he said, alerting Liam and Amir. "Unidentified vehicle heading our way."

He put down his cup and picked up his gun. Then he waited for the vehicle to approach and prepared to stand his ground.

ELEVEN

Brent stood at the kitchen window, gun in hand, waiting for the car to arrive at the house. Ducking from view and shielding his eyes from the dazzling headlights, he tried to get a good look at the vehicle. It was big and black, with shiny hubcaps gleaming in the night. As it ground to a halt on the gravel outside the house, Brent decided that now was the time to act.

He burst through the door with his gun out front, aiming for the windshield. Then he yelled an order.

"Get out of the car with your hands in the air."

The engine was cut but the occupants remained inside. Liam appeared at his side with his weapon directed at the car.

"Amir is standing guard upstairs," he said. "Who's in the car?"

"I don't know." Brent edged his way across the crunchy gravel. "They won't get out."

He and Liam made their way toward the dark vehicle. The driver was completely still, staring straight ahead beneath a baseball cap. Brent didn't recognize him.

"Get out of the car!" he repeated. "Otherwise, I'll shoot out the tires."

The back door of the SUV opened and a man was pushed from the vehicle. He fell onto the ground with a heavy thud. Brent pointed his weapon in response to the threat, but the man didn't move. He looked to be dead. And around his neck was a sign that read SNITCH. The door promptly closed again and the car began to reverse.

Brent aimed for the front tire. "Stop the car."

As the driver failed to comply, Brent put a bullet in the rubber. A loud bang echoed around the fields and once again he repeated his order for the occupants to exit the car. Liam tried to open the passenger door but it was locked, and the driver remained impassive in his seat, hands curled around the wheel. It appeared that he was being given orders by somebody in the back, but the darkened glass at the rear of the vehicle prevented a full assessment of who might be pulling the strings.

The car began to pick up speed, still in Reverse, the flat tire thumping rhythmically as it turned. Liam put a bullet in the passenger-side front tire, but still the car didn't stop. The engine was revved hard and the vehicle accelerated, before the driver performed a hand-brake turn in the middle of the lane, sliding on the gravel and kicking up stones. Then it sped toward the main road, its hood dipping low on the flat front tires.

Brent holstered his gun. "Call the emergency FBI line and ask them to get here immediately. I'm going after that car. It won't get far on those tires."

A series of bullets rang out from the vehicle, causing Brent and Liam to dive to the ground. When Brent dared look up, he saw two men exit the damaged car and get into a black Corvette that had been waiting at the side of the highway. The deep throaty engine roared to life and the sports car took off. Its taillights rapidly disappeared into the darkness. There was no point in pursuing now. Brent would never succeed in catching them. Instead, he picked himself up and dusted down his clothes, before walking to the lifeless body that had been dumped in front of the house.

"I guess this must be the informant," he said, pointing to the SNITCH sign. "Dumping his dead body here is obviously meant to send us a message."

"I think it's literally meant to send a message, boss," Liam said, plucking a white envelope from the man's pocket. "This has got your name on it."

Brent took the envelope and read the block capital letters written on the front: SHERIFF BRENT FOX, CHILD STEALER.

By the time dawn had broken, the FBI had removed both the body of the informant and the abandoned black car. A special agent now sat in the living room of the safe house, discussing Brent's options with him, but urging him to enter a witness protection program with his children.

Special Agent Moranis was a mature man who looked like he'd seen plenty of action in his time. He rose from his seat to walk to the window, checking on the police guards who had been stationed outside the house.

"The man who was killed and dumped here last night was named George Davola, and he was the informant who'd turned on Kendall Buchannan."

"I guessed as much," said Brent. "I thought he was in protective custody."

"He was, but he was stupid enough to change his mind. He got cold feet and decided to withdraw his testimony. Then he left his secure location and returned to Buchannan to ask for a second chance." The agent sucked in air through his teeth. "Kendall Buchannan does not give second chances."

Brent looked up as Carly came downstairs and entered the room. She had kept out of the way since the danger had unfolded, but had constantly checked on Noah and Ruby, who had thankfully slept through the entire night. As they now waited for the children to awaken, Liam and Amir were catching up on their sleep. And as for Brent, he was exhausted but wired. He wanted to learn all the facts of the case before showing the agent the letter that had been left in the dead man's pocket.

"Who doesn't give second chances?" Carly asked, having clearly caught the end of the conversation.

"Buchannan," Brent replied. "He brought a dead man to the house last night."

"Correction." Special Agent Moranis held up a hand. "He brought two dead men to the house last night."

"Two?" Brent was confused. "Who was the other one?"

"Clarence Odell," Moranis replied. "We found him in the trunk of the car. He'd been hog-tied and shot in the back of the head."

Carly's hand flew to her mouth and Brent patted the seat next to him on the couch. She came over and sat close to him, leaning her shoulder against his. They were using each other for support, and he was glad.

"Odell had obviously outlived his usefulness," Moranis continued. "Now that Buchannan is no longer being monitored via an ankle tag, he obviously wants to take over the abduction attempts himself. The Bureau has been trying to take down Kendall Buchannan for a very long time. When he got his tag removed and the murder charges were dropped, we tried to keep a tail on him, but he switched himself for a decoy and we lost him. If we can get enough evidence from the car, we'll be able to rearrest him for this double homicide."

"And attempting to abduct and traffic children outside US borders," Brent prompted.

"All of our current evidence against Buchannan came from the informant. Now that he's dead, we have nothing to put on an arrest warrant."

Brent was incredulous. "Are you kidding? He's made several attempts to abduct my children."

"Did you ever see Buchannan try to snatch your kids?" the agent asked. "Did you see him last night? Have either of you even seen him in the Pinedale area? We just don't have the evidence to make that charge stick, even though it's true."

Brent reached into his pocket and pulled out the envelope. "Buchannan left me this note last night, which makes his intentions pretty clear."

The agent took the envelope and pulled out the letter. While he read the contents, Brent gave Carly an overview.

"Buchannan wants me to deliver the children to a private airport close to Jackson at midday today. He says if I don't comply, he'll kill you while making me watch."

"Seriously? He honestly thinks you'll give up your children because of a murderous threat?"

"According to him, Noah and Ruby are not my children, so giving them up should be easy."

"He wishes you weren't their father," she said angrily. "You're more of a dad to Noah and Ruby than he could ever hope to be. His idea of fatherhood is centered on control and bullying."

Special Agent Moranis sat in an armchair. "This letter contains some very serious and credible threats, Sheriff Fox. If Buchannan wants you to deliver the children to an air-field, then he has plans to fly them out of the country immediately. It would appear that he's given up on trying to gain access to his baby son, who's already in protective custody, so Noah and Ruby have become his main focus now."

"He's not taking them." Brent spoke through gritted teeth. "There's no way on earth I'd let that happen."

The agent nodded in agreement. "We'll have a team of agents waiting to arrest Buchannan at the airport today. Meanwhile, I advise you and Ms. Engelman to accompany me to an FBI safe house where you'll be protected twenty-four hours a day. The children will of course come too." He looked between Brent and Carly. "We'll keep your family together."

The agent had assumed they were an item, and Brent didn't correct him. He *did* feel as though they were a family, and this gave him a sense of comfort.

"How do we know the FBI safe house won't be discovered?" Brent asked. "This place was a secret from everybody except my pastor, and he didn't breathe a word. Until we know how Buchannan found us, we won't be safe anywhere."

"Can you be sure that you weren't followed at some point?" the agent asked. "Or maybe you overlooked a tracking device in a car or bag?"

"No," Brent replied. "We've been incredibly careful since Odell managed to put a tracker in the car we borrowed from the police. We check everything thoroughly."

"Well, Buchannan found you somehow, so it makes sense to allow the FBI to take the lead. I'll draw up an arrest warrant based on this letter and we'll take him into custody."

Brent didn't share the agent's enthusiasm. "I just don't think Buchannan will be stupid enough to show himself today. He'll be prepared for a potential double cross because he must realize that I won't give up my kids without a fight. He's bound to send one of his cronies instead of being there himself."

"We won't know until we attend the meet," the agent said. "Until then, the best course of action is for your family to come with me."

Ruby's voice floated from the top of the stairs. "Daddy Brent?" she called. "I need the bathroom and Noah peed on the seat."

Carly stood up. "I'll go deal with it. You stay and talk with Agent Moranis."

The agent smiled at Brent as Carly left the room. "I have two kids myself," he said.

"They're adults now, but I remember those days when they were small and needed me all the time. They grow up so fast, so I recommend you enjoy every day."

"I'm trying," Brent said. "It's not easy when a madman is determined to hunt us down."

He wondered how much longer he would have to wait to relax and enjoy family life. He was desperate to begin his role as a legal and permanent father to his children, but he had been thwarted at every turn. He didn't want to hide away in protective custody for an undetermined amount of time. He wanted Noah and Ruby to go back to school, to return to playdates and sports clubs, to enjoy time with their friends like other kids.

Brent also wanted Carly to share in their family life with them. Maybe she would agree to stay in touch. Perhaps she would even come over for dinner on occasion. The thought of continuing their lives without her was hard to contemplate. He would have to broach the subject with her when the time was right. If the time was ever right.

Carly came back into the living room and pointed to the kitchen area.

"We're just getting some juice from the fridge," she said. "We'll take it upstairs."

Ruby, holding Carly's hand, padded across

the carpet in pajamas and bare feet, clutching the stuffed bunny from the cabin.

"Why is that man wearing church clothes?" Ruby asked, looking at the agent in his shirt and tie. "Is it Sunday?"

"Yes, it's Sunday, but we can't go to our church service today, sweetheart," Brent replied. "God won't mind if we skip a week because we're dealing with lots of important things."

Ruby didn't take her eyes off the agent. "Is he your friend, Daddy?"

"He's everybody's friend, and he's here to take us to a new house, because this one isn't quite right for us."

Agent Moranis crouched down and waved. "Hi. My name is Robert, but you can call me Bob."

"My name is Ruby," she replied. "You can call me Ruby."

Special Agent Moranis nodded very solemnly. "I'm pleased to meet you, Ruby." He touched the stuffed rabbit. "Is this a friend of yours?"

"This is Bugsy." Ruby pulled the rabbit close, defensively. "He only likes me and he goes wherever I go."

A sensation of iciness washed over Brent, as though he had jumped into a winter lake.

How had he been so stupid? How could he have allowed this to happen?

"Ruby, can I take a look at Bugsy for a moment?" He reached for the toy. "I think he might have something in his tummy that's making him sick."

Ruby looked at him with concern. Then, with the complete trust of a child responding to a parent, she handed the bunny to Brent and followed him into the kitchen as he took out a pair of scissors from the drawer. While three pairs of eyes watched, Brent cut a hole in the toy's heavily padded stomach and poked a finger into the white stuffing. The tracking device was instantly found, and he teased it through the tear in the fabric with his thumb and forefinger.

He kept a cool composure, not wanting to spook or upset his daughter. "I knew that Bugsy had a tummy problem," he said with a smile. "But now everything will be okay." On seeing her crestfallen face, he added, "We'll sew him up so he'll be just like new."

As Ruby went to the refrigerator to take out some juice, he dropped his voice low and explained the situation to the agent.

"Ruby took this soft toy from her bedroom at the cabin. We assumed it belonged to the judge's granddaughter, but Odell must've placed it there as a precaution. He knew his plan to abduct the kids right from under our noses was risky, so this was his fail-safe in case he had to abandon the attempt. Odell would've known that Ruby can't resist Charlie Bear toys." He clicked his tongue in annoyance. "I should've realized it was planted on the shelf."

"It's a child's stuffed animal, Brent," Carly said. "None of us thought it was sinister."

As Ruby tugged on Brent's shirt and handed him the carton of juice to open, he picked her up and held her in his arms, kissing the top of her head and tickling her chin. She squealed in delight, oblivious to the danger that had been only a few feet away just hours ago.

And that was the way he intended it to stay.

Carly could see that Brent was anxious. He was pacing the deck while the agent loaded bags into the car. He looked exhausted, having not slept for the entire night. He needed to crawl into a warm bed and close his eyes, but he was fueled by adrenaline and coffee.

"We're almost ready to go, Sheriff," Agent Moranis said. "It's a long journey so we'll make a couple stops along the way."

Brent stood up straight and placed his hands on his hips, as if he'd made a sudden decision.

"I'm not going," he said. "I have a plan."

"A plan?" Moranis said with obvious concern. "Do you want to share it with me?"

Brent dug into his pocket and pulled out the stuffed rabbit's tracking device. They had intended to destroy it right before leaving the safe house. Once the tracker lost its signal, Buchannan might dispatch men to the house in order to follow them, so the agent decided to delay deactivating it until it was too late.

"This is still transmitting a GPS location, right?" he said, holding up the small black box. "And Buchannan doesn't know we've found it. That means he'll follow the signal, because he'll assume it's still inside the stuffed rabbit."

Carly could see where he was headed. "And if he follows the signal, you'll be ready and waiting for him."

He snapped his fingers. "Bingo!"

Agent Moranis puffed out his cheeks. "I wouldn't advise using yourself as bait. There are too many things that can go wrong. Buchannan might attack when you aren't expecting it. He might bring an army of men with him. He might even get wise to your plan. It's a bad idea."

Carly disagreed. "It's a great idea. But you'll need somebody with you."

"No." Brent stood firm on this. "I'll do it alone. I'll return to the cabin in the woods to deal with Buchannan once and for all. Otherwise, I'll never be rid of him."

Carly was incredulous. "You're exhausted, Brent. You'll need somebody to drive you there and stand guard while you get some sleep. You can't do it on your own."

Agent Moranis went one step further. "You shouldn't do it at all. There's a very good chance that you'll end up in serious trouble, and you'll be miles away from the emergency services. It's a terrible location and a terrible idea."

"I appreciate the advice," Brent said. "And I understand your concerns, but I'm familiar with the cabin's layout and location. I'm confident that I can outsmart Buchannan if he turns up."

"And you don't think he'll smell a rat?" the agent asked. "After all, Odell already found you there just a few days ago."

"Buchannan is acting like an irrational man right now. I honestly don't think he'll try to second-guess me. Once he pinpoints the tracker, he'll go tearing up there without thinking it through. His impetuousness will work in my favor."

Agent Moranis raised a skeptical eyebrow.

"I still don't think you should go rogue. You could end up regretting it."

"I'm not going rogue," Brent said with a small smile. "As a sheriff, I don't go looking for trouble, but if trouble comes my way, I'll take whatever action necessary. I'm not breaking the law."

Agent Moranis returned Brent's wry smile with one of his own.

"As a father, I admire you. As an agent of the FBI, I disapprove."

But Brent's mind was apparently made up. Carly knew him well by now, and she could tell that he wouldn't back down. And neither would she. Buchannan had terrorized her for days and threatened to kill her while forcing Brent to watch. She didn't want to hide away and wait for somebody else to make the danger disappear. She wanted to tackle it head-on. With Brent by her side, she felt she could conquer anything. But he would never agree to her accompanying him.

Brent shoved the tracker back into his pocket. "I'm Noah and Ruby's father and it's my job to neutralize anything that might hurt them. I know you'd like me to play by the rule book, Agent Moranis, but I'd never forgive myself if I ran away like a coward to wait for Buchannan to find us. If you'll transport

Noah, Ruby and Carly to a safe house until this is all over, I'll be forever in your debt. I won't even ask where you're taking them because if I don't know the location, I can't reveal it, even under torture."

The agent let out a long and weary sigh. "I can't prevent you from going anywhere you wish to go, Sheriff Fox, although I should be logging that GPS tracker as evidence."

Brent covered his pocket with his hand. "What tracker?"

The agent narrowed his eyes. "Just return it to me when you're done with it. I'll take one of your deputies as a guardian for the children while they're in the care of the FBI. My priority right now is securing them in a new location."

"Carly can also be their guardian while I'm away," Brent said. "They adore her and feel safe with her."

"I'm okay with that," she said with a forced smile as she prepared to tell a big lie. "But I need to meet up with a US marshal first. He's meeting me at Evergreen Gas Station."

"Really?" Agent Moranis was naturally surprised. "Why? And why didn't I know about this before now?"

"The marshal called me on my cell a few minutes ago," she said. "He apologized for the early call, but he needs to see me urgently regarding a child abuse case I'm currently involved with." She thought she should elaborate on the lie, so she relied on her basic knowledge of the US Marshals' jurisdiction. "A mother and child had to go into a witness protection program, but they've gone missing. I might be able to provide vital information to track them down."

"You can't do it over the phone?"

She had to think on her feet. "He wants me to look at some mug shots in person. It's complex."

"And he's meeting you at a gas station? Are you sure of his credentials?"

"Of course. I've met him quite a few times already."

Agent Moranis pulled out his cell. "Give me his details and I'll check him out."

She waved away the concern. "There's no need. And no time. He'll be waiting for me already, so we should leave. He's relying on me to help with his investigation."

Moranis shook his head, before saying what Carly had been counting on hearing. "We can't stop along the way to the safe house. It breaks protocol."

"Can I go into Pinedale with Brent and then have the marshal take me to the safe house afterward?" she suggested. "That sounds like the best solution, right?"

Moranis reached into his pocket and handed her a card. "Have him call me once you're done. We'll send a car for you. And don't leave his sight until we get there, okay? If you already know this marshal, you'll be safe with him."

She took the card. "Okay." She slipped it into her pocket, knowing she would never need a car to come for her. Step one of her plan to accompany Brent to the cabin was now in place.

Brent held Noah and Ruby in his arms while kneeling between them. Their little bodies were warm and limp, and their arms around his neck felt wonderful. He had told them they were going on an adventure with Uncle Amir and Carly while he went away on a short trip. They had naturally assumed his trip was related to their adoption in some way, and Brent saw no reason to correct them. Their innocence was beautiful and he wanted nothing to spoil it. When they were adults, he would explain the situation to them, but for the time being it was important to allow them to be children.

"Are you going to see the judge?" Noah asked. "So that you can be our real daddy?"

"Hey." Brent touched Noah's nose with the tip of his finger. "I already am your real daddy. We don't need anybody else to tell us that, right?"

"If you're our real daddy already, then can we choose a mommy too?" Noah asked.

Brent closed his eyes for a brief moment, wondering how to respond to this heartfelt question.

"I choose Carly," Ruby said with a huge smile. "Definitely Carly."

Brent looked up at Carly, who was standing next to them. She crouched down and tucked a strand of Ruby's hair behind her ear.

"I really love you both very much and I'll always be in your lives." Brent saw her quickly wipe away a tear. "Of all the children I've ever met, you two are the bravest and kindest."

"Noah isn't brave," Ruby said with a shake of her ponytails. "He's scared of the monsters under his bed."

"I am *not*," Noah shot back quickly. "I only have a night-light because I don't like the dark."

"Listen to me, both of you," Brent said, holding them a little tighter. "You two are brother and sister, which means that you take care of each other when Daddy's not around.

We're a family, right? And families aren't perfect, but they show love to one another."

"Okay, Daddy," Noah said. "I'll look after Ruby. And I'll always lift the seat on the toilet."

Brent laughed. "You're a good boy. You both make me very proud." He glanced across at Carly, who seemed to be trying to hide her tears. "Pretty soon, we'll be able to change your surname to Fox, and then we'll get a cake to celebrate."

Ruby let out an excited scream into Brent's ear that forced him to turn his head away.

"Ruby Fox!" She jumped up and down. "It sounds like a cuddly toy. I LOVE it!"

Carly began to laugh as she reached for a tissue in her jeans pocket to dab at her eyes. "Isn't it amazing how the smallest things mean the most to kids," she said. "Ruby wouldn't care if you had all the money in the world. What matters to her is that you're turning her into a stuffed animal toy."

He laughed along. "I gotta admit, it wasn't the reaction I was expecting."

Amir's shadow fell across them. "It's time to go, boss," he said. "Do you have everything you need?"

With one final kiss on the foreheads of his

children, Brent stood up and guided them to take Amir's hands, one on each side.

"Yep," he said. "We're good to go. Take care of them, Deputy, and we'll see you soon. Carly will be with you later today after meeting with the marshal."

With a nod of his head, Amir led Noah and Ruby to the waiting car of Special Agent Moranis, while Brent looked on, reassuring himself they were in safe hands. The Bureau was equipped with resources that he simply didn't have, and their location would not be compromised by tracking devices. Nevertheless, seeing them leave was difficult, and he rubbed at his chest, where a twinge of pain arose.

He felt Carly's hand slip into his and squeeze. It was physical contact that he badly needed at that moment, and he squeezed back as the agent's car set off down the lane. When it turned onto the highway, Liam pulled away from the curbside in his deputy's cruiser to escort the children to their new location. Having now returned to duty, Liam was the ideal person to perform this important task, and Brent silently gave thanks for the men who had stood by him since danger had darkened his door. But Brent was now actively entering the danger zone and he didn't feel comfortable placing them, or Carly, in the firing line. He wanted to act alone, and as soon as he delivered Carly into the safe hands of the US marshal, he could finally put an end to Buchannan's campaign of terror. Or at least that was what he hoped.

Carly's plan worked out perfectly. After she'd offered to drive into Pinedale, Brent had fallen asleep almost instantly. She'd known that he would. He was exhausted after staying up all night. While he was unable to object, she'd sailed right past Evergreen Gas Station and headed on up to Fremont Lake, enjoying the beautiful views in spite of the dangerous situation.

Born and raised in Cheyenne, Carly was much more used to the city than a rural setting, and she had never been much of a person for the great outdoors. But her move to Pinedale might just change all that. The Wind River Mountain Range offered so many opportunities to immerse herself in nature, from wooded hills to deep valleys. There were also lakes and glaciers, as well as vast areas of wilderness in which to hike. It was the perfect place to raise a family, where children could learn all about how to respect God's spectacular creation. It was where she could raise a child of her own and give them all the benefits that came with being part of a strong community.

Brent stirred beside her.

"Where are we?" he asked. "We're miles away from the gas station." He looked around in panic. "We have to go back."

"No, we don't," she said calmly. "Because I'm coming with you."

"Oh no you're not. You're meeting the US marshal like you promised."

"I made it all up, Brent," she said. "There's no US marshal and there are no people who've gone missing from the Witness Protection Program." She kept her eyes on the road, but she knew he was staring at her with an open mouth. "I'm sorry that I lied, but I couldn't let you go back to the cabin alone. I want to be with you."

When he failed to respond, she began to worry that she'd gone too far.

"Say something," she urged. "Anything."

"If we turn back now, we might have enough time to call Agent Moranis to send a car for you. How long was I asleep?"

"A couple hours," she said. "I took the scenic route to give you some time to rest."

"And to make sure I couldn't mess with your plan, huh?" He sighed. "Too much time has passed to safely turn back. Without knowing Buchannan's whereabouts, we can't risk it. We'll have to let Agent Moranis know that you'll be accompanying me instead of going to the safe house."

She stole a glance at him. "Are you mad?"

"Yes. No. I'm not sure. I'm kind of honored that you'd do this for me, but I wish you hadn't. I care too much about you to place you in danger."

"But it's my choice," she argued. "We should be together."

"Should we?" he asked. "Why?"

"Well…" She stopped, uncertain how to put her feelings into words. "I can't explain it, but I'm letting my heart lead the way."

"I see." He scratched at his bristly neck. "I guess I can't argue with that kind of logic."

She laughed, glad that he had decided to lighten the mood. She didn't want any animosity between them, because they needed to work as a team to defeat the threat heading their way. All she knew in that moment was that she belonged by his side.

Brent wasn't sure what to think or how to feel. Carly had rejected the security of the safe house to remain with him. Did this mean that she cared about him in the same way he cared about her? Did she love him? Or was he reading too much into it? Whatever her reasons for doing what she did, he couldn't help but feel glad for her presence. She was right—they belonged together.

As they got nearer the cabin, he realized that he hadn't praised her for her bravery.

"Thank you," he said, touching her shoulder. "You could've chosen the easy option, but you stayed with me. That kind of loyalty is hard to find. Tamsin was the only other woman who would've sacrificed her safety for me."

Carly shifted awkwardly in her seat. "Tamsin was your wife. It's a no-brainer that she would've stood with you when you faced danger."

A silence descended as Brent realized what Carly's actions were saying. She was displaying the devotion and love that he'd associate with a marriage vow. Yet they weren't even dating. They'd shared an amazing kiss, but that was where their relationship ended.

After an uncomfortable minute had passed, Carly could clearly stand the silence no longer.

"Tamsin was obviously a special person and you loved her a lot." She turned off the main road and onto the dirt track that led to the cabin in the forest. "You might be fortunate enough to find somebody who gives you goose bumps again."

He hesitated before replying, as his skin tingled with actual goose bumps. "I'd like to get married if the right woman wanted the same thing."

The tension in the car ramped up a notch, and he wondered what Carly was thinking.

"And what if the right woman *did* want the same thing?" she asked finally.

He turned his head to look directly at her. "Then I'd get down on one knee and propose."

"I see." She concentrated on navigating the bumpy track. "Well, I sure hope she says yes."

TWELVE

Brent walked down the stairs of the cabin and was greeted by the smell of cinnamon and coffee. After their arrival, he had called Agent Moranis to update him on the situation and then gone to bed for another couple hours to make sure he was fresh and clear-minded for the day ahead. He suspected that Buchannan wouldn't launch an attack until the midday deadline had passed and the clock was just approaching that time now.

The cabin was exactly as they'd left it, with the key still under the flowerpot on the porch. Brent had been in touch with the county judge, who had readily agreed to his vacation home being used for the purposes that Brent intended. And his intentions were very clear in his mind: to take Kendall Buchannan into custody and force him to face justice for terrorizing his family.

"Hi there," Carly said brightly as he entered the kitchen. "I baked some cinnamon buns that I found in the freezer. They're still warm." She pushed a plate of freshly risen dough across the counter. "And I worked on your case while you slept. I've written to my boss, recommending that Kendall Buchannan be legally prevented from claiming any paternal rights over Noah and Ruby. If we can get this approved by a court quickly, then there's no need to delay the finalization hearing. I don't foresee a problem, because it's in the best interests of the children."

He sat on a stool at the counter. "You've been amazing throughout this whole process. Thank you."

She shifted on her feet. "That's not true though, is it? I haven't been amazing. For a lot of the time, I've been a pain in the butt."

He took one of the buns and began to peel away a layer of sweet cinnamon dough. "I was being too polite to mention it."

She smiled and placed an empty cup in front of him, before pouring coffee from the pot.

"I'm sorry if I was hard on you," she said. "I didn't know you very well at the start of the adoption procedure, and I wanted to be sure."

He took a swig of his coffee. She really didn't need to apologize to him for being unable to let go of her fears. If only she had opened up to him earlier, he'd have understood her reticence and been able to help.

"I know why you acted the way you did," he said. "You went through a very traumatic experience and you were motivated by a desire to stop all children from being hurt. Your heart was in the right place, and that's all that matters."

She sat opposite him at the counter, cradling her cup. She was wearing a hooded sweatshirt in a deep shade of red, and the color contrasted vividly against her blond hair. Even with no makeup, she was strikingly beautiful. He couldn't help but stare.

"After Laurie died, I stopped overseeing adoptions entirely," she said. "I thought I was protecting myself from pain, but all I was doing was depriving vulnerable children of an advocate."

"Does that mean you've changed your mind?"

"Definitely. When I emailed my boss, I also submitted a request for a return to adoption cases. Heaven knows, children in the care system need a bossy woman like me on their side."

He laughed. He didn't think his admiration for her could grow any bigger. When she had first agreed to accompany him and the children to a safe house, she was bitter at the world and angry with God. His patience had been pushed to its limits by her defensiveness and prickly exterior. To see her sitting in front of him, having shed all of the pain and negativity, brought him great joy. She had worked hard to accept the past and move forward with a sense of purpose. He had always been drawn to strong women, and she certainly fit the bill.

But what struck him as more remarkable than any of this was her willingness to put herself in danger for the sake of his family. She could be sitting in an FBI safe house now, allowing others to take the strain in tracking down Kendall Buchannan. Yet, she was here with him, seemingly calm and unafraid.

"Why did you come here?" he asked impulsively. "We're literally using ourselves as bait. You could be playing games with the children right now. Or you could even have gone home."

"I don't have a home, remember?"

He made a face. He'd forgotten about the fire at her apartment. "It's not possible to transport you to the safe house, but you could get a room for the night. We passed a motel that's only a few minutes away. Even though we want to be together, I'd feel much more comfortable if you weren't here."

She made swirling motions with her forefinger on the countertop, as if she was nervous or self-conscious.

"I don't want to go anywhere, Brent. When you suggested I go home, it gave me a weird feeling. I've never really thought of my apartment as my home, not even before I moved to Pinedale," she said. "It was just a place to eat my meals and go to sleep, before returning to work in the morning. It wasn't until I started spending time with you and the children that I realized what a home should feel like."

Now he was super interested in what she was saying. "And what should it feel like?"

She took a deep breath and let it out with a gentle sigh. "Like two strong arms that hold you tight." She closed her eyes and hugged herself as if imagining it. "Home is a place where you can be yourself among people who love you, even on your worst days. It's kind of like a church, I guess, because the building itself doesn't matter. The people inside the house turn it into a home."

He steeled himself to ask a question he was worried would overstep his boundaries.

"Do *I* feel like home?"

She opened her eyes. "Yes."

He smiled. This surely was an affirmation that she could see a future for them as a couple. When he'd spoken in the car about settling down with the right woman, he wasn't sure if she'd realized that he was talking about her. He'd given up fighting the attraction. He didn't care if her workplace disapproved of the relationship, or if folks thought he was moving on too quickly after losing his wife. He loved her. Nothing else mattered.

"You feel like home to me too," he said, reaching across the counter and touching her hand. "I love you."

She looked down at his hand atop hers and slowly slid hers from beneath. She didn't repeat the words back to him, and his heart sank into his belly. Had he gotten this all wrong?

"Did I move too fast?" he asked. "I just wanted you to know how I feel."

"I'm not sure how things would work between us," she said. "I've recently started to make plans for my life and I don't know whether you'd fit into those plans. There's a lot to consider."

He was prepared to fight for her. "The only way we'll figure it out is if we talk it through, right?"

"I don't want to force you into a difficult position. You have a family to think about."

He guessed she must be referring to her desire to adopt a child from the care system. He was definitely open to the idea of expanding his family. His excitement rose at the thought of a new addition to his tribe, and with Carly by his side his life would be complete.

"I adore kids," he said. "So if you're worried about your plan to adopt, then you should know that I'm on board."

She looked at him with a disbelieving expression. "That's a huge commitment to make on the spur of the moment, Brent. You should take some time to think about it."

"What's to think about? I love you." He shrugged. "It's a no-brainer."

As his cell began to buzz in his pocket, she slid off the stool and made her way toward the door, as if determined to force him to find an obstacle to their relationship. He pulled his phone from his jeans and held up his hand to get her attention.

"Let's put this conversation on hold," he said. "Because there's plenty more that I want to say."

Throughout the day, Carly thought about her conversation with Brent. Could it really be that easy for Carly to fall in love and live happily ever after? Brent had been open and honest about the strength of his feelings, so why couldn't she be in return?

Because she wasn't sure he understood what he was getting himself into. Carly's plan was to adopt a child who was most in need of a loving parent. This would almost certainly involve dealing with behavioral issues and past trauma. Children like this were always passed over for adoption, time and time again. She'd seen it firsthand. Watching these kids grow up in the care system made her want to weep. She wanted to shout from the hilltops that neglected and challenging children were worthy of love and affection just like everybody else. On those rare occasions when a deeply traumatized child had found an adoptive home, they had blossomed and thrived. Carly even had a child in mind—a ten-year-old boy named Jackson who had been in care for five years and had given up hope of ever finding a mom and dad. His angry outbursts had deterred all potential couples, but she saw through the bravado, all the way through to his frightened and lonely center.

"It's getting dark." Brent came into the living room, where she sat by the window, watching the trees beyond the front yard for signs of danger. "We should get ready."

She stood up. "I have my gun and cell phone with me, and the flare gun is by the back door."

"Good. Keep your gun on you at all times. I can't stress this enough. Don't leave it in a purse or on a table."

She nodded. "I understand."

"We know that Buchannan didn't show himself at the airport earlier, so he's still out there, and he's almost certainly heading our way right at this moment."

Brent's phone call earlier that day had been from Special Agent Moranis, letting him know that no arrests had been made at the airport due to the fact that no suspects had been identified. Most likely, Buchannan's men had been watching from afar, instructed not to make a move until certain that Noah and Ruby were present.

"Remember," Brent said. "You need to let me face the danger. Once Buchannan thinks I'm dead and he goes into the decoy room, we barricade the door and call for backup. If he sees a bunch of officers heading this way before he's trapped, he'll hightail it out of here and we'll have achieved nothing."

"Got it."

On the coffee table were the essential items required for their plan to work. First, there was Brent's bulletproof vest. It was bulky and uncomfortable, but it would allow him to take a bullet to the torso and leave nothing more than a bruise behind. Second, there was a name plaque to hang on a bedroom door. Brent and Carly had spent an hour with the craft supplies, spelling out Ruby's name on a small wooden board, using buttons and glitter. It was the kind of thing a child might create, so Brent hoped it would appear authentic.

"Do you really think this will work, Brent?" Carly asked, eyeing the items on the coffee table.

"It's a simple plan, but I'm confident. If anything goes wrong, you head out deep into the woods with the flare gun and call 911. They'll find you by following the flare. I can take care of myself."

She grabbed his hand, suddenly overcome with a need to tell him what was in her heart.

"I love you, Brent. I'm sorry I couldn't say it earlier, but I didn't know whether you'd be on board with adopting the child I've chosen. It's a big commitment."

He cupped her cheek. "You can ask me later, because right now I see car headlights coming down the track. It doesn't even look like Buchannan is trying to hide because he thinks he has the element of surprise." He handed her the name plaque and picked up his bulletproof vest. "Let's get into position."

She pressed her lips onto his and placed a hand on his cheek. He responded by holding her close and whispering into her ear.

"Stay safe, because we have a life to plan after this is over."

Brent sat at the kitchen table with the light dimmed low. Meanwhile, Carly was hiding upstairs waiting for Buchannan to take the bait. It was likely that Buchannan would be angry after Brent's failure to deliver the children, and this could work to Brent's advantage. Angry men usually didn't think straight. They got sloppy and made mistakes. That's what he was relying on this evening.

He heard the car pull up outside the cabin, and voices filled the air. He thought he heard two, or maybe three, men. As he'd suspected, no knock on the door came. Instead, it was busted open with a firm kick from a boot. Buchannan's silhouette filled the open doorway, dressed in army fatigues, like he was cosplaying a soldier. Quick as a flash, Brent bolted from his position and out the back door.

He heard Buchannan's order just as his feet touched the grass of the backyard.

"Kill him."

This was what he had hoped for. It was the reason he had worn a white sweatshirt. In the darkness, the bright fabric would provide a perfect target for a gunman. He slowed his pace, giving time for his attacker to come within reach before he entered the cover of trees. When the bullets hit him, Brent didn't need to pretend to fall. The force of the blows took him clean off his feet and he sprawled to the earthy ground, sliding in the leaves and taking in a mouthful of dirt. Then he lay perfectly still, hands outstretched, as three dull throbs pulsed in his back. His gun rested loosely in his palm, with his index finger curled around the trigger.

"I got him, Buck," the man yelled with apparent glee. "Three times."

Buchannan wasn't satisfied. "Well, go make sure he's dead. I'm heading upstairs."

Brent remained still, waiting for the footsteps to come closer, crunching through the leaves leisurely. When he was certain of the man's position, he flipped onto his back and fired a shot in a split second. His attacker was frozen in a posture of surprise, his mouth forming an O shape as blood oozed from his neck. With another well-placed shot, Brent took him down.

Then he jumped up and ran, making his

way into the house, spitting the dirt out of his mouth. Buchannan would assume those two gunshots had come from his accomplice's weapon and would have no reason to suspect anything was amiss. Now, all Brent needed to do was finish the plan he'd started. Entering the house through the back door, he heard cursing and wailing from upstairs, followed by the *pop-pop-pop* of a gun. It sounded like stage two had been implemented.

Vaulting the stairs two at a time, Brent arrived on the landing to see Carly desperately trying to drag a heavy dresser across the door of the decoy room.

"He's inside," she said. "I locked the door, but we need to get the barricade in place. He's shooting the lock."

It had been Carly's idea to use a name plaque on the door to lure Buchannan into a large closet on the second floor of the cabin. With no windows through which to escape, his only exit would be blocked, and he'd be contained. Brent rushed forward to help her, but her eyes widened in horror as she looked at something beyond his shoulder. That alerted him to the danger. A second accomplice was there with them.

Brent swung around and raised his gun, only to find it knocked from his hand. His assailant was armed, and Brent fought to take his weapon from him, but they were both strong and evenly matched. As they rolled over and over on the rug, Brent caught sight of Carly still trying to push the dresser across the door by herself. But she wasn't able to drag it into place, and Buchannan's last bullet finally broke the lock. He emerged onto the landing, screaming at the top of his voice.

"Where are my children?"

Buchannan pushed Carly so hard against the wall that she was badly winded. While she struggled to regain her breath, he pinned her by her neck, bringing his face close. His features were contorted with rage.

"Where are my children? If you don't take me to them, I'll shoot your arms and legs and leave you in the woods to bleed out." He plucked her gun from the waistband of her pants as she tried to reach it. "I'll even use your own gun."

She gasped for air, her eyes never leaving Brent and his attacker, who were fighting for supremacy on the floor.

"In there," she croaked, pointing to the bedroom that had been hers. "Both in there."

He let go of her neck and she dropped to the floor with a thud. The plan had gone awry and she didn't know what to do. Brent would want her to flee into the woods with the flare gun, but she wouldn't leave him. She knew with certainty right there and then that she would never leave him. He looked to be gaining the upper hand in his tussle, so she needed to buy him some time and prevent Buchannan from joining forces with his accomplice. With a quick and desperate prayer to God, she followed Buchannan into the bedroom and watched him tear off the sheets from the bed as he sought out Noah and Ruby.

"LIAR!" he yelled, spinning around and taking aim at her with her own gun.

As gunshots sounded in the hallway, she wondered whether they had come from Brent's gun, or if he was in trouble. With no time to go check, she picked up a heavy vase from the dresser beside her, and, finding superhuman strength, she hurled it through the air. It hit the large window behind Buchannan with a huge bang, shattering the glass on impact.

He looked at the broken pane in apparent amusement. "You missed."

A familiar voice filled the air. "I don't think she did."

Brent appeared behind her and fired his weapon over her shoulder repeatedly. The shots were deafening, and she covered her ears with her hands, watching Buchannan being pushed backward with each bullet. Unable to regain his footing, he staggered on his feet, his face a perfect mixture of shock and confusion. Brent gave him no time to take aim of his own and walked calmly forward, placing one final bullet to send Buchannan falling over the low sill and toward the window. Carly watched him scrabble at the edges of the frame as he realized what was happening, but it was too late. He tumbled through the large gap with a yelp of anguish.

She didn't rush forward to watch the impact, but she heard it well enough. Brent crunched over the broken glass and peered at the scene below, grimacing at the sight. Then he pulled his cell phone from his pocket and placed a call to 911, requesting assistance from his deputies.

"My guys will be here as soon as they can," he said, wrapping her in his arms. "It's over. It didn't quite go as planned, but we found a way."

"That's what I love about you." She wiped away a spot of blood on his lip. "You always find a way."

He took her hand. "Let's go outside. I've got something I want to say."

* * *

The night sky was clear, with a bright moon that could almost make Carly forget the terrible danger that had visited them that evening. But the three dead bodies that lay in and around the cabin were reminders of that danger. Those men had lost their lives because they had chosen to steal children from a father who would stop at nothing to protect them. In the far distance, Carly could see the red and blue lights of the sheriff's deputies' vehicles. She reckoned she and Brent had five minutes, maybe ten, before the whole place was crawling with uniforms.

She sat on the porch step, and Brent laid a blanket from the swing chair across her shoulders. Then he sat next to her and took her hand. His eyes glittered in the moonlight, a warm and flecked hazel, with a frame of dark lashes.

"Did I ever tell you how amazing you are?" he asked.

She smiled. "Yes, but I don't mind if you want to tell me again."

"I know that neither of us expected to end up falling in love, but I'm so glad it happened."

"Listen, Brent—"

He cut her off, obviously preempting her

concerns by quashing them before she could voice them.

"I would love to adopt a child with you," he said. "And I don't mind who that child might be. Noah and Ruby are my children, no matter what their biology says, and I'll feel the same way about any new addition into my family. If the child is from a traumatized background, then I can promise you that we will make the hurt and pain go away. Love heals all wounds, especially those of children."

A lump formed in her throat. "Really? Are you sure?"

"I'm sure. When I'm with you, I feel invincible."

She touched his lip. "You're bleeding. You're definitely not invincible."

He pulled a tissue from his pocket and wiped away the blood. "It just needs to be kissed better, that's all."

She placed a hand on his cheek and pulled his face to hers. She kissed his lips gently and tenderly, and he responded by winding his fingers through her hair at the nape of her neck. When he finally pulled away, the lights and the sirens had grown much closer.

"Your deputies will be here in a couple minutes," she said. "Is there anything else you wanted to say?"

He made a big show of appearing to think carefully. "I don't think so."

She bumped her shoulder into his. "Are you sure?"

He snapped his fingers, as if remembering an important detail. "Oh yeah! There *was* something else."

"Well, hurry up, because we don't have all night."

He stood and walked down the two porch steps to stand on the ground. Then he got down onto a bended knee and placed a flat palm across his heart.

"Carly Engelman, would you do me the greatest honor of agreeing to be my wife?"

She nodded her head in a combination of enthusiasm and excitement. "Yes, I would."

He got to his feet and held his arms out wide, with a huge, beaming smile on his face. In a rush of hot tears, she jumped up and threw herself into his arms, after which he spun her around until she was dizzy and breathless.

Not only had she found a man she loved, but she'd found a ready-made family. The Lord had blessed her in ways she'd never expected. And her gratitude knew no bounds.

EPILOGUE

Eight months later

From her elevated bench, the judge looked down at the confetti on the carpet and wagged a finger at Carly, who had just tossed it into the air.

"I'll tolerate the mess in my courtroom just this once because it's such a special occasion." She relented under the smiling faces of the family in front of her and rose from her chair to give them a round of applause. "You deserve to celebrate, Sheriff and Mrs. Fox. I hope your family enjoys a lifetime of happiness together. Your journey toward adoption has come to an end. For now, at least."

Carly placed an arm around the newest member of the family: Jackson, the eleven-year-old chatterbox and skateboard fanatic, who had joined the Fox family household six months ago, right after Noah and Ruby's adoption decree had been signed. After marrying Brent in a beautiful ceremony in their Pinedale church, Carly had made her own court application to adopt Noah and Ruby, and had now become their legally appointed mother. Jackson was the icing on the cake, bringing her and Brent's brood to three, with each of the children possessing their own unique personalities and characters.

"Let's gather together for a photograph," the judge said, heading their way. "This is always my favorite part of the finalization hearing."

Brent kissed Carly on the forehead. "Happy adoption day, honey." He then ruffled the hair on Jackson's head. "Now you're stuck with us forever, buddy."

Jackson wrapped his arms around Brent's waist and rested his head on his new father's torso. Carly bit her lip to stop the tears from flowing. This young man had overcome incredible hardships in his life to learn to trust adults again. His integration into the family hadn't always been smooth sailing, and a lot of therapy had taken place, but he had settled in well after accepting their love. He even called Brent and Carly Mom and Pop, which was music to their ears.

"I want a hug too," Noah said, tugging on Jackson's sweater. "Me next."

Jackson let go of Brent and playfully punched Noah on the shoulder. "Now that I'm your official big brother, you have to give me all your stuff, including the dinosaur fossils on your dresser."

Noah was wise to Jackson's teasing. "And you have to let me ride on the handlebars of your bike when you go to the park."

Carly held up a hand. "Nobody is doing that, ever, especially without a helmet." She patted Jackson on his back. "Now give your little brother a hug like he asked."

As the boys embraced, she pinched Ruby's cheek. Her daughter was now sitting in Brent's arms, wearing a Disney princess outfit that included an elaborate dress, silver tiara, costume jewelry and glittery cape. Ruby was going through an obsessive phase, so most everything in her bedroom and closet was princess themed.

"How are you doing, Princess Sparkles?" Carly asked. "All okay?"

Ruby squirmed to be put onto her feet. "I want to go over there." She pointed at the judge. "And talk to Darth Vader."

Carly and Brent covered their giggles with their hands.

"I'm sorry," Brent called to the judge with a shrug. "It's the black robe."

The judge took it in stride and crouched down to speak to Ruby, explaining that they would now all pose for a photograph to remember the day, but sadly no light sabers were available as props.

"This is our first photograph as a court-appointed family of five," Brent said wistfully, holding her close.

She leaned into his ear and whispered, "Actually, it's six."

"The judge isn't part of our family, honey." He made a face. "And you know I love you, but I'm *not* adopting a sixty-year-old lady."

She took his hand and guided it to her belly, where the very first beginnings of a swell were taking shape. His eyes widened in sudden surprise.

"What?" He was disbelieving. "How did this happen?"

She tilted her head. "I think you know how it happened."

Their plan hadn't included a biological child, but life obviously had other ideas. Carly knew that whether a child was birthed by her or adopted through the courts, it didn't matter to either of them. Each child would be loved and treated equally.

Brent rubbed at his smooth chin. He had recently shaved his beard, and Carly found that it suited him. He looked younger and more handsome than ever.

"We're gonna need a bigger house," he said. "And a minivan." He slapped a hand to his forehead. "Oh boy, I've become one of those men who drives a minivan."

"Plenty of rugged men drive minivans," she said, smirking. "With princess stickers all over the windows."

He puffed out his cheeks. "My deputies will revoke my sheriff badge when they hear about this."

She threw back her head and laughed. There was never a dull moment between them, and Brent constantly had her in stitches with some silly story or terrible joke. Dinnertimes were always hilarious, and Carly adored being in the bosom of a rowdy, noisy and affectionate family. Her solitary life had changed beyond recognition.

"Liam loves to watch *My Little Pony* with Ruby," she said, smoothing down Brent's shirt collar. "I think your sheriff badge is perfectly safe."

He quickly kissed her on the lips as the judge arranged the children in height order, ready for the photograph to be taken.

"All joking aside, this is amazing news," he said. "I can't wait to tell the kids."

"About the baby or the minivan?"

"The minivan, of course. It's the most exciting thing that's ever happened to us."

"Let's go, mister wisecrack." She led him by the hand to stand behind his assembled children. "Our family is waiting."

* * * * *

Dear Reader,

I do not have any experience of fostering and adoption, but I came across many personal stories while undertaking online research. People who choose to open up their homes to the most vulnerable children are truly living by God's word. Adopting an older child can be especially challenging, but enduring love has the power to change that child's life immeasurably.

Every child should feel loved and protected by their parents, but sadly this doesn't always happen. And this is where women like Carly Engelman deserve a huge amount of respect and admiration. Children's advocates, just like Carly, step onto the front line of a battlefield every day, ensuring that the smallest in society do not suffer because of their parents' actions. I salute them all.

Brent and Carly are both fierce protectors who find common ground in their values. Their shared principles lead to love, as they realize that they make a sparky match. As parents, they make a superb team, which is why I wanted to grow their family at the end. It was such a satisfying conclusion to write, and I hope you enjoyed every step of their story.

Thank you for being one of my valued readers.

Blessings,
Elisabeth